Acclaim

"There are a lot o[...] [...]
Much Heart, but these aren't gruesome tales. Bodies — or just
the parts—are handled in the same straightforward manner as
the arrival of a pizza and Oreos before bedtime, a high-stakes
Pogs game. And when things go full-on surreal, all remains
quite normal. In fact, everything is just fine here in *So Much
Heart*. I'm not sure what to call this ultra-realistic surrealism,
but I love it and I love these stories."

—Mary Miller, author of *Biloxi* and *Always Happy Hour*

"You're the kind of honest that happens when you're lonely.
You're late-night driving through Texas with a stranger—a
pizza delivery guy for Papa John's. It's humid, unhinged, but
hopeful. In *So Much Heart*, Drew Buxton pulls us close to
losers and rejects, and we recognize ourselves. We scratch each
other's backs."

—Ashleigh Bryant Phillips, author of *Sleepovers*

"*So Much Heart* drips authenticity with every sentence, in
every story, within this high-spirited collection. Drew Buxton
somehow manages to take bizarre feelings buried deep inside
of us and make them into buoyant tales that we can all relate
to on a deeply personal level. He makes the awkward, okay.
The odd, feel casual. And erratic human emotions something
to be celebrated, not shunned. In short, *So Much Heart* is the
ultimate vibe check for everyone who reads it. Whether you
pass is up to you."

—Mallory Smart, author of *The Only Living Girl In Chicago*

"Buxton's stories read like that shot in Lynch's *Blue Velvet* where we push past the green grass of Norman Rockwell Americana and see the rotten, cruel underbelly of things. Corpses, recess, cockfights in Vegas—these stories feel like cinema. *"I want to tell him how, sometimes when I'm alone in the house, I shit my pants on purpose."* Funny, unnerving, and gothic, these stories feel like blood relations to Donald Ray Pollock, Amelia Gray, or Stephen King."

—Oliver Zarandi, author of *Soft Fruit in the Sun*

"Drew Buxton's stories are a joy: surprising, keenly observed, and—truth in advertising!—full of heart. An exciting new writer to watch."

—Michael Hingston, editor, *Short Story Advent Calendar*

"I don't know that I've ever read stories quite like the ones housed inside this collection—a surreal, vivid, and entirely unpretentious blend of Saturday morning cartoons, absurd horror, and manic realism. There are jokes in these stories that, years after reading for the first time, still make me laugh out loud when I think of them, and little grace notes of humanity that still cross my mind at odd hours. This thing rules."

—Chris Vanjonack, has an agent

"Drew Buxton's stories are full of cheap beer, dead bodies, failed therapies, and the throes of addiction. But, in all this doubt and darkness, he never fails to show us the humanity at the center. Buxton's stories are relentlessly compelling."

—John Dermot Woods, author of *The Baltimore Atrocities*

SO MUCH HEART
STORIES

Drew Buxton

MMXXIII

www.withanxbooks.com
Cover Design by Huff Stuff
Layout by Jon Nix
WAX005
ISBN 979-8-9874787-2-1

For Dad

I gotta tell you — I started out pretty strong and fast, but it's beginning to get to me.

— Lucas "Cool Hand Luke" Jackson

Lexapro

We did the photo shoot outside the Austin OCD Center. The staff took pictures of me and Scott. They took pictures of us sitting in the garden and standing with the big house behind us. We went back inside and changed into different clothes, and they took more pictures. It was an exposure, and our SUDS (Subjective Units of Distress) went through the roof. The idea is that you make yourself anxious on purpose so you get used to it and realize you can take it. I got up to an eight. Scott was being hilarious and making faces and saying ignorant shit like, "These hos ain't ready for Scottie Too Hottie." The pictures were for our Tinder profiles.

Scott didn't like how his turned out. He said he looked fat. He wasn't fat; he had body dysmorphia, but we had put on some weight since we got to the program, no doubt. There was this cookie place that would deliver, and every night after treatment, Scott would say, "We deserve it, all the hard work we're doing." He was like the voice inside my head come to life. The Lexapro they had me on made me hungry all the time, and the place had these red velvet cookies.

For his profile, Scott used old pictures where he was skinnier. He said if he matched with someone hot, he would lose the weight really fast before they met for a date. I looked fat in my pictures too, but I didn't care about that. That wasn't why I couldn't make my profile. I didn't think I deserved a girlfriend and thought none of the girls would like me if they knew all the terrible things I'd done. I had memories of hurting people, hitting people with my car, etc. With OCD, you can't tell if memories are real or not. I wasn't allowed to watch the news or call the hospitals to check for hit-and-runs. The staff said I just had to live with the uncertainty and move forward. I had thoughts of killing my boxer, Ellis, and I'd gotten rid of all the knives in my house. The staff had me walk around with a butcher knife in my pocket.

After the treatment day ended at 4 p.m., Scott and I went outside to play basketball in the driveway. As an exposure, he had to play with his shirt off. I took mine off too to support him. He had a little belly, but mine was bigger. We played pig and around the world, and my fat bounced each time I took a jump shot. I think it helped Scott to see my body because he started joking around. He flexed and said he was Brock Lesnar, the professional wrestler. He grabbed the ball and tried to crush it in his hands. He couldn't do it so he punted it over the fence into the neighbor's yard. He laughed like a maniac.

That night Scott connected his iPhone to the living room TV. The staff and the other patients sat on the sectional, and we watched him go through his Tinder. One of the girls had a lot of makeup on and was obese. Her eyebrows looked like they were drawn on with a marker. "Look at this ghoul!" Scott said and laughed his crazy laugh. He didn't know any better. He was about to turn twenty. He zoomed in on her face. "It's a creature feature!"

"You're terrible," one of the staff said. She was laughing too. Everyone was laughing.

He turned to me and said, "That was really bad, wasn't it?" He wasn't smiling. "Oh my God." He unplugged his phone and got up and walked up the stairs. We called for him to come back, but the staff told me not to go after him. He had to experience the shame and guilt and not do any rituals like getting reassurance. I knew his SUDS were out of control.

I wondered if it was bad to laugh at people on Tinder. I had moral scrupulosity OCD, and I wasn't supposed to try to figure out if stuff was right or wrong. It would send me down an endless spiral. I made an uncertainty statement like they taught us. *It may or may not be wrong to make fun of people on Tinder, and I'm okay with not knowing.* It was getting easier. I could tell the Lexapro was helping.

I asked for my meds and started getting sleepy. I headed up to my room, and it was quiet upstairs. I knocked softly on Scott's door. He hadn't hurt anyone, I thought. There wasn't an answer. We weren't allowed in each other's rooms, but I slipped in and shut the door behind me. The room was dark, but I could see that the bathroom light was on. "Scott," I said. "What happened?"

13

"I can't believe I said that. I'm disgusted with myself."

"Which part?"

"That ghoul comment."

"It's okay. We know you were joking."

"Is that sexist, you think?"

"I don't know."

"She was kinda ghoulish, huh?" he said and laughed. Then there was a pause. "You know how many matches I've gotten?"

"How many?"

He opened the door and stepped out. "Fucking zero." He went to his bed and sat down. His face turned serious. "It's honestly got me down."

"You just gotta be patient."

"I've never had sex," he said. "I just want to have sex."

He looked down at the floor, his hands pasted to his thighs, and asked me if I was nervous my first time. He asked what it felt like. He asked how many people I'd been with. He asked if I'd ever measured my penis.

"Mine is four and a half inches. Is that bad?" he said and looked up at me.

I told him I wasn't sure that it mattered. He stood up and said he wasn't sure he could be naked in front of another person. I knew I'd already given him too much reassurance.

* * *

They had me do a driving exposure in the staff van. I drove around Hyde Park, and every time I hit a bump, I wasn't allowed to look in my mirrors to make sure I hadn't hit anybody. Maybe I did, maybe I didn't. Afterwards, I had to sit on the couch and stew in the uncertainty. They made sure I didn't turn on the news.

Scott sat down on the other couch and took his phone out even though we were supposed to turn them in every morning before treatment started. He said he'd upgraded to Tinder Platinum. "It's twenty bucks a month, but I already got a match." He showed her to me. She went to UT, and she had a picture with a Lab mix. It triggered my harm OCD about Ellis.

"She's cute," I said. Her name was Georgia.

That night we gathered on the sectional, and he put his Tinder back on the TV. We talked about what his first message to Georgia should be. We agreed he should compliment her dog. I said he should write, "Somehow you're even cuter than your dog." I wasn't serious but he loved it and I couldn't talk him out of using it. The staff encouraged him.

It worked somehow and Georgia wrote back, *aw thanks*. I felt jealous and knew I had to get my profile ready. The staff had been asking if I'd done it yet. I wanted to have sex too.

"She likes you, Scott!" one of the staff said.

"She's thirsty," another said.

Scott suddenly got shy and disconnected his phone from the TV. "You guys are making fun of me," he said and stomped up the stairs. We let him be.

* * *

The next morning they served us eggs and bacon. Scott took his fork and pushed his onto my plate. He said Georgia didn't like texting back and forth and wanted to meet up soon. He had to get skinny quick. "To buy some time, I told her I was going to be really busy with school for the next couple weeks," he said. He wasn't in college anymore. He'd told me he failed out because the OCD had gotten so bad he never left his dorm room, couldn't risk saying the wrong thing to someone. I think there was other stuff going on too though. We all had other stuff going on. I was depressed. I was a financial advisor at a credit union, and I told them it was about mental health. They told me to take all the time I needed. They were so scared of discrimination lawsuits.

We had morning group in the garden, and the leader guy talked about how everyone has intrusive thoughts. Everyone has wild sexual and violent thoughts that pop up and leave, but with OCD people get stuck on them and an emergency signal gets fired from the amygdala. I was next to Scott on the bench, and he whispered that he was having intrusive thoughts about stabbing me and setting my body on fire. I told him I was thinking of castrating him and putting his genitals in the garbage disposal.

When group let out, they had me print out pictures of Ellis and post them all over the house—pictures of him as a puppy, sleeping and rolling around on the ground. It was a constant exposure. I put one on my bathroom mirror, one by the TV. When I walked past them, I didn't ruminate, and I repeated out loud, "I may or may not kill my dog. There's no way to be sure." It was crazy but it started to work. The rumination started feeling not so automatic. It would be a new start for me and Ellis, and I decided to rename him Lexapro, Lex for short. He was only two, and I read online that it's more about the tone you use than the name itself.

He was still young and would catch on fast.

They were pushing Scott with his exposures too. They added stuff to his behavior plan like getting naked in front of someone. They said getting naked in front of a friend was a good way to build up to eventually being naked in front of a sexual partner.

One day after lunch, we went up to his room. I sat on his bed, and he stood with his back to the wall. He took his shoes and socks off and then his shirt. He barely had a belly at all. The crash diet was working, but his face looked gaunt and sucked in. I asked him where his SUDS were, and he said an eight. He undid his belt and slowly pulled down the zipper of his jeans. He slid them down to his feet and kicked them off. He let out a deep sigh. He was in just his boxers. "I can't," he said.

"It's okay. Good job," I said. He was progressing.

He set up a coffee date with Georgia, and on the day of, he was a mess. He'd already had too much coffee that morning and it was hot out. He was sweating through his polo shirt. "I'm so horny," he said. "She's so hot." He was looking at her Tinder profile again. I got him to eat a bowl of cereal just to have something in his stomach. The place was walking distance from the Center, and we wished him good luck. He started to walk off but then turned around and asked if he looked fat, but we didn't answer.

I was still struggling with the dating stuff, and the staff was losing patience with me. They'd give us our phones back in the afternoon after therapy ended, and one day I noticed that Tinder had been downloaded. I'd gotten even bigger since we had the photo shoot in the garden and needed new pictures. I didn't want to be a catfish. It's just I felt the need to confess my thoughts. It was a compulsion, and when I started confessing to staff, they'd just walk away or ignore me. I thought it was wrong to not tell the women what kind of person they were dealing with. I felt like I should put it on my profile: *I may or may not kill my dog*, but they wouldn't let me.

We rushed up to Scott when he came through the door a few hours later, asking him how it went. He said it was great. "It was like we knew each other from before," he said. "There weren't, like, any awkward pauses or anything." They were gonna hang out again soon. We were all happy for him, and it made me feel like I could do it too.

That was the final test for Scott. The next day they told him he was ready for discharge. I knew it had been coming. He'd been getting better faster than me. On his last night, we ordered cookies one last time. We sat on the couch and ate them with tall glasses of milk. The sugar made him hyper, and he said he wondered what it was like to give a blowjob. "Not like I'm gay, but I wonder how it feels." He got a banana from the kitchen and tried to deep throat it. He got it about halfway in then gagged. I knew I was gonna be so bored without him.

It was almost 11 p.m. when we had to go upstairs, and we were crashing from the sugar. He said, "I wanna tell you something, but I'm not sure if it's a confession." I knew that if you weren't sure, it probably was. That's what I told him.

"Whatever. I don't care. I gotta tell you. I didn't meet Georgia."

"Really? Where did you go?"

"I went in the coffee shop and saw her. I couldn't go up to her so I just went to the bathroom. I don't think she saw me. I hid in a stall for thirty minutes and jerked off looking at her profile pictures."

"Christ. Did she message you?"

"Yeah, but I didn't read it. I deleted my Tinder after."

I told him it was still a step in the right direction. At least he'd set up a date. I still hadn't set my profile up.

* * *

The next morning Scott's parents came to pick him up. I gave him a hug, and he blew me a kiss from the car as they drove away. We joked about how it was going to be quiet and boring without him, and it was. We felt it immediately. Morning group had no energy, and I had nothing to distract me from the intrusive thoughts.

After the treatment day, there was no one to play basketball with, so I sat on the couch and opened Tinder. I had to own that I wanted a girlfriend and not get lost in whether I deserved one or not. I didn't know what to put for the bio so I asked one of the staff for help. She sat down next to me.

"What do you like to do for fun?" she asked.

I sat there and thought. I liked to watch TV, well, I liked to have the TV on. It was hard for me to focus.

"Do you like to go outside, like hiking?"

"Not really. I walk around the neighborhood sometimes."

"That counts as hiking, I think." She told me to put it down even though it wasn't totally honest. It was for my therapy—doing morally gray things and then not ruminating about them. I went with it and also wrote that I liked to read. I saved my profile, and the staff wouldn't leave until I started swiping.

* * *

With Scott gone, I focused harder on treatment. I wanted to get out of there. I spent my evenings on Tinder. I started just swiping right on every girl, and I got some matches. We talked and they said my dog in the picture was cute. It triggered me but I kept talking. The staff started bringing in their dogs from home. I had to hang out with them while I went about my day. I walked them around Hyde Park and wondered if I was strangling them with the leash. My SUDS stopped spiking and rarely got over a six. They told me I was good to go. I'd been there just under six weeks.

Before I left, we had cupcakes, and staff went around the room and each said something about me. They said they'd seen me grow so much since I first got there. I wasn't sure. I thought maybe it was just the Lexapro.

I went straight from the Center to the boarder to pick up Lex. He was excited to see me, and the bad thoughts came and hung out. Would he still love me if he knew I thought about putting him in the oven? I called him Ellis by accident, and I felt bad because I know it confused him.

That night I made a stir fry. I cut up the steak and heard Lex's nails clack on the kitchen tile. I squeezed the knife and felt its weight. He pawed at my leg. I cut the excess fat off the slices and set the knife down. I told Lex it wasn't for him and to get out of the kitchen, but he kept coming back to my feet, hoping a piece might fall.

So Much Heart

For a few weeks after he jumped out of that plane, D.B. Cooper took up more space in the paper than Vietnam. Mom read the front page while hanging on her crutch and smoking her Camels. Even with her leg in a cast, she didn't like sitting too long. She shook her head. "They'll never catch him," she said. "Probably in Canada by now." She hobbled over to the den, looking for something.

"What do you need?" I asked.

She pointed at her UFO magazine on the coffee table. It sat on old Moon Pie wrappers, all dusted with cigarette ash. I handed it to her, and she dropped onto the couch. It'd been a month since she fell out of a deer blind and broke her leg in three places. She'd been drinking, I knew. "Time for you to get going," she said.

I finished my Kix fast and got my jacket and hat from the coat closet. I grabbed the Canon from the fireplace mantel and took two film cartridges.

"Now, Collin, that was $120," Mom said. She always reminded me how much it was.

I went out the front door and walked in the middle of the dirt road, away from the tall grass, like Mom said to, so anyone coming would see me, usually hunters and fishermen in pickups. Shelley's house was the closest house to us, right before the road ended. It was a country house a little off the road. It didn't have a second story, but it was big. I went down the path to the gravel yard. Shelley's mom kept it bare without any decorations, but I could see their Christmas tree through the window, all lit up. Christmas was only two weeks away.

The door was never locked, and I went inside. Shelley must've heard me. She came running from the den, smiling. "Let's go catch a sasquatch!" she said.

"You don't catch a bigfoot," I said. "We're trying to get one on camera."

"Whatever." Shelley didn't know what she was talking about.

We went outside and started into the woods, down the thin hunting trail.

"You better stay behind me," I said. "In case he jumps out."

She didn't listen and skipped ahead.

"It could happen," I said. I kept the camera ready. It could happen anytime, like how Bigfoot just walked out in front of Patterson and Gimlin while they were riding horses.

Shelley hummed, and I shushed her and said we had to be as quiet as possible. I warmed up from all the walking around, and I took off my jacket.

"Yeah, I'm hot now," Shelley said and took hers off too. She had a sweater on underneath, and it lifted up for a second and showed her stomach. She saw me looking, and I had to say something.

"It's not far to the end of the trail," I said and walked fast.

Once we got there, we started through the bushes and huge sequoias and moved slow on the muddy ground.

"I'm bored," Shelley said.

"I can't go back yet. Another half hour," I said. Mom would get mad if I came back too early.

Shelley sighed. "Did you bring any snacks?"

I felt my pockets even though I knew there was nothing in there. "No, noth—" I started to say before I smelled something. I covered my nose with my sweatshirt sleeve. It was rank, worse than anything, like something rotten. "Do you smell that?"

"Gross," Shelley said. They said Bigfoot smelled terrible and that you'd smell him before you saw him. My feet felt stuck in the mud.

"He's close," I whispered.

"What?" she said and laughed. "Who is?"

"Don't laugh." I took a deep breath. I brought the camera up and hit record and turned slow in a circle. The smell had me shook up. I couldn't tell which direction it was coming from.

I crouched down and waved for Shelley to do the same. She smiled and sat down cross-legged. I listened close— nothing.

"Stay," I whispered to Shelley and stood and tiptoed forward. I went between the trees and spotted something

23

about ten yards away, on the sprawling roots of a sequoia.

It reflected the little bit of sun that got through, and I heard flies buzzing. It was something leather, a brown leather jacket. The flies got worse as I got closer. There were black pants too, legs. It was a person. I backed up three steps. I picked up some rocks and threw them at him. He didn't move.

I took off and yelled "Run!" and flew past Shelley. We ran until we got to a small clearing and were out of breath. I put my hands on my knees. Shelley was giggling.

"What was it? Did you get it on camera?"

I shook my head. I noticed the Canon was still running and turned it off.

"Was it a bear?" she said.

"No. It's a guy, but he's..." I felt like I couldn't say it out loud, like it was a cuss word.

"What?"

"He's dead."

Shelley covered her mouth with her hands. It was quiet.

"We gotta tell our moms," I said. "They can call an ambulance."

"Yeah, but I wanna go see first."

I was scared but kinda wanted to go see it again. We covered our noses and mouths, but it didn't make a difference, and the smell stung our faces. The body was curled up in a ball.

"You go closer," I said.

"You go. I dare you," she said. I handed her the camera and took little steps. He was on his side, turned away from us. I walked around and saw his face. There were holes where his eyes had been eaten out, and his mouth was gaping open and full of flies.

I stepped backwards then tripped on my feet and fell on my butt. I got up and backed away.

"What?" Shelley said. I tried to talk but couldn't. I pointed at the head, and she came over, covering her eyes with her hands. I pulled her hands down. We stared at him.

"He's dead," Shelley said. He'd died like how animals die. He seemed young, with a full head of brown hair. I thought death only happened to people like Great Granny, hunched over with bumpy skin.

"He's dead," Shelley said again.

"Yeah." I bet no other kid in the fourth grade had ever seen a dead body before. I'd tell everyone when we got back from Christmas break.

I snapped out of it and looked away. There was something a few yards away, a brown briefcase. Shelley saw it too and went and dragged it away from the body.

"It's heavy," she said.

"Don't open it," I said for some reason but knew we had to. Shelley undid the latches and opened it and stepped back. I reached down and grabbed a chunk and tried to feel if it was real. It was money, one-hundred-dollar bills. The briefcase was full of them. I'd never seen one before. I didn't know who the guy with the long hair was.

"We're rich," Shelley whispered.

I looked back at the body. The leather jacket. I looked up in the trees, and there it was, a mangled parachute. No way. They said he'd jumped somewhere by us, the Oregon-Washington border.

"It's D.B. Cooper," I said.

"No!" Shelley said and went over to him and leaned in

close.

"It's gotta be," I said.

"It looks like him. Oh my God."

"There's $200,000 in that briefcase," I said. That's the ransom he'd asked for. That's what the paper said. The cops said he couldn't have survived, the way the weather was that night, rainy and freezing. Mom said the cops were only saying that because they were embarrassed he got away. She was rooting for him.

"We're rich," Shelley said again and came up close to me and took my hands. "My mom is gonna freak out."

"Mine too. Everybody's looking for him, but guess who found him?" I turned the camera on and filmed him and the money. I pictured Mom when I showed it to her. She'd call the news and we'd be on TV and in the paper. She'd love it. I thought about the cops. They'd be everywhere. They'd interview us and collect the evidence—take away the body and the briefcase.

"No," I said and turned off the Canon.

"No what?"

"We can't tell our moms."

"Why not?"

"Because," I said. "I don't know. Think about it. It'll mess everything up. Everyone will come here, the cops and everyone. They'll probably take the money."

"But we found it," Shelley said.

"I know, but I dunno. Let's keep it a secret for now."

We needed to get back for lunch, so we hid the briefcase in some bushes and started back. "I want a bike for Christmas," Shelley said.

"Me too." There were lots of bikes in Mom's catalogs.

I liked the blue Schwinn that cost $79.99, but Mom kept warning me not to expect much for Christmas. I knew money was low since she'd switched from Budweiser to Glacier Light.

"My mom keeps this one room locked so it might be in there," Shelley said. "I tried to look under the door but I couldn't see anything."

* * *

When I got home, I told Mom there was nothing to report.

"It's tough," she said. "They're more active at night."

She'd already started drinking, the coffee table filling up with beer cans. She kept drinking coffee too, switching back and forth. She made tuna salad but forgot she already added mayo and added more. I made a sandwich even though it was gross.

"What if the cops are right?" I asked.

"About what?"

"D.B. Cooper. What if he didn't make it?"

"After everything he went through, I don't think some rain was stopping him."

"Yeah," I said and made myself take a bite. "It was storming bad that night though. Remember?"

She waved her hand at me. "We're talking about a guy who didn't just hijack a plane. He had the nerve to land it, get the loot, then take back off." She laughed. "*Then* jump out of the goddamn thing! You know how much heart that takes?"

"What would they do with the money though?" I said. "If he didn't make it and someone found it."

"What'd I just fucking tell you?"

* * *

I waited until after dinner to ask if I could spend the night at Shelley's. We always did sleepovers at Shelley's. I waited until Mom started slurring and smoking her Camels back-to-back. We watched a rerun of *Bonanza*, and she kept dozing off until her cigarette burned her fingers and woke her up. When I finally asked, she said, "I don't care."

She was out for good when the credits rolled, and that's when I smelled it and jumped up from the couch. A dark spot grew on her gray sweatpants. It'd been a while since she peed herself, since before Great Granny died, when we'd done Thanksgiving at her place and they kept opening bottles of wine.

I left quiet. I didn't want her to think I'd been there for it. I pictured her with her cast, having a hard time cleaning it up, getting mad and cussing.

It was totally dark out besides Shelley's porchlight down the road. When I walked in, she and her mom were sitting on the carpet by the coffee table, working on a new puzzle. They were always doing puzzles, and her mom would get them framed and hang them up. Her mom smiled and waved me over. "Reinforcements have arrived!" she said. She was a nice lady. She was skinny with long brown hair and glasses. She worked as a secretary at a law office in town, and she kept the house clean.

The puzzle was of the solar system and was mostly black. They'd already done the border and the planets, so it was at the hard part. I pretended like I was trying, picking up pieces and pressing them together. I couldn't wait to talk to Shelley alone. I was worried about someone else stumbling across the body and money.

After a long hour, Shelley's mom stretched out her arms and yawned and made a show of getting up from the floor. "I'm going to bed," she said and told us we could have three Oreos each and that she knew how many were in there. After she walked through the kitchen and turned the corner, Shelley held her finger to her lips. We waited a little.

"My mom said the cops would take the money," I lied.

"Mine too. I've been thinking about it. We've got to get rid of the body."

"We can hide it," I said.

"No," she said. "We have to bury it. The money too."

She was right. We decided to go first thing in the morning. We went and got our Oreos and dipped them in milk. "I'm not tired," I said.

"Me neither."

I thought about the briefcase sitting there, exposed.

"I won't be able to sleep," she said. "Let's just go now."

"I want to but—" I didn't want to admit I was scared.

"What?"

"Bigfoot is more active at night."

She laughed. "C'mon, you really believe in Bigfoot?"

"Yeah. There's video of him."

"My mom said that's a guy in a monkey suit."

"My mom said when her leg is better, she's gonna shoot one so no one will be able to say they're not real."

Shelley sighed. "We'll be careful," she said.

Her mom had a shovel in the garage she used for the gravel outside. It was heavy, but I was strong, and we found

29

a flashlight too. We put on our winter stuff and went out the back door because it made less noise. We were as bundled up as we could be, but the wind still cut through. We took turns carrying the shovel over our shoulders.

It was too cold to talk as we went down the trail. The wind blew the odor at us as we got close, and we found him after wandering around for a while in the dark. The flies were gone.

"It needs to be a real burial," Shelley said. The trees were close together, and roots ran everywhere. There wasn't a good spot to lay him out flat.

"We'll have to do it in the clearing," I said. We decided to bury the money first. We took out $500 each and stuffed the bills in our pockets. We figured that would last forever.

The ground was wet and soft, but I still had to jump on the shovel to really dig. It was hard work, and after a while, Shelley grabbed the shovel and put her hand on my back. We took turns like that until it was about a foot and a half deep. That was good enough for the briefcase, we thought. We had to be able to get to it easy.

We went to the clearing, and I started digging the hole for D.B. I didn't feel cold anymore. I thought about that cop who came to our class last year and said you should always call the cops if you see someone doing something bad or if someone is hurt. I asked Shelley if she remembered that.

"Yeah."

"What about his family?" I said. "Don't you think they're worried?"

She didn't answer, and we didn't talk for a while. We dug and dug, and I pictured Mom's face when she saw the money, and I imagined riding the Schwinn down the trails.

Shelley threw the shovel to the ground. "I quit," she said. The grave was about a yard deep. We had no idea what time it was, but it was still pitch-black out.

We went back to where he was, and Shelley told me to grab a foot. We'd drag him. I was so tired I didn't care that much, but I made sure to only touch the black sock and not the skin. It felt loose around the bone. We counted to three and pulled as hard as we could and moved him a little each time.

* * *

I woke up gripping my sleeping bag tight. I laid still on my stomach, and the sun shone through the window. Shelley was up already. I could hear them talking in the kitchen. We'd gotten back while it was still dark, and I fell dead asleep as soon as I laid down.

I sat up and felt my thighs were wet. I kicked the sleeping bag away and felt myself. I smelled it. I'd peed myself, something I hadn't done since first grade. I went into the hallway and opened the front door.

"Collin?" Shelley's mom yelled, and I took off. It was cold. I forgot my jacket, but I kept running until I got home, and I waited outside the house until I caught my breath.

Inside, Mom was drinking her beer and coffee. "Where the hell did you go? I thought you were upstairs sleeping."

"I spent the night at Shelley's, remember?"

She shrugged, and I went to the pantry, but there weren't any Kix left.

"We're out of cereal," I said.

"Make a sandwich."

31

"There's no bread either. You gotta go to the store."

"I gotta go to the store? You know what?" she said. "Here's something *you* can do." She wrote something on the newspaper and tore it off and held it out for me. It was a phone number.

"That's your dad's number. You can tell him we're out of bread and cereal and everything else because I damn sure haven't seen a dime from him lately."

I put it in my pocket and felt the bills. I wanted to take them out and throw them up in the air. I took the peanut butter from the pantry and got a spoon and went upstairs to my room and started crying.

* * *

That afternoon, I pretended to call my dad in front of Mom. I dialed the number but changed the last digit. A woman picked up and said "Hello" a few times then hung up.

"He didn't pick up," I said.

Mom rolled her eyes and shook her head. She was mad at him now instead of me and seemed like she was in a better mood. Before dinnertime, I asked if I could spend the night at Shelley's. She said, "Of course," and took my face in her hands and brought me in close. "Honey, I'm gonna be on my feet real soon and back at work. We'll be fine. We're always fine in the end." She smiled. I turned to go, but she held on. "Right?"

"Yeah," I said and smiled back even though I wasn't sure what she meant.

Shelley's mom made meatloaf and mashed potatoes and green beans and let me get seconds. It was hard for me not to doze off afterwards while we worked on the puzzle. After Shelley's mom went to bed, we talked strategy. There was still a week left before Christmas. I thought about just leaving the money by the front door for Mom to find. Not knowing how it got there would drive her nuts, though, and she'd have to figure it out.

"When we were in the woods, you were talking about his family," Shelley said. "I've been thinking about it. You think his mom is looking for him?"

"Yeah. She has to be, if she's still alive." I wondered if all moms lived as long as Great Granny did. I wondered if he told her what he was gonna do.

After a while, Shelley came up with a plan. We took her mom's typewriter out onto the back porch so we wouldn't wake her up with the hacking. Shelley knew how to type. She wrote a letter saying the money was a reader giveaway from *UFO Magazine*. We laughed. Mom would be so excited she wouldn't question it.

We went back inside and put the typewriter back in its place on the desk. I was giddy. There was a little mud hill right when you went into the woods that I could use as a ramp.

We sat on the couch and tried to think of a plan for Shelley's mom. She said maybe it could be a Christmas bonus from her boss.

"But what about when she thanks her boss and he doesn't know what she's talking about?"

"Oh yeah."

We kept thinking until Shelley said she was tired and ready for bed. She didn't seem that worried about it.

That night, I had a dream that I was on the plane with D.B. All the passengers were gone. We'd let them go when we picked up the ransom. It was just us and the two pilots up front. The stairs were down, and we were looking into the black, stormy night. I was dressed up like him with sunglasses and a leather jacket. I told him I was so scared. He smiled at me and said he was scared too, but he knew I could do it. It was just the jumping part that was hard.

* * *

In the morning, I brought the letter in with the rest of the mail and set it on the kitchen counter. "A lot of mail," I said, trying to sound normal. Mom didn't move from the couch. I went and sat next to her.

"You got a letter, I think," I said.

"Oh yeah? Bring it over then."

I gave it to her and tried to keep my eyes on the TV. She stared at the letter, reading it over and over. She peeked into the envelope. She looked up at me, and I turned away. She pulled herself up with her crutch and went upstairs to her bedroom.

She was singing something when she came down an hour later and got a beer from the fridge. She said we were going into town later for dinner. She played the radio and danced in her chair. She told me to get myself a beer, and I jumped off the couch. It tasted nasty, but it made everything funny. I got into the music and laughed at Mom's dancing.

Around dinnertime, I heard the rumbling of a diesel engine outside and knew it was Clyde.

"There he is!" Mom said. "Honey, run and get the door."

Clyde had thick brown hair parted down the middle and a thick mustache. He had a case of Glacier Light in his hand.

"Hey, little dude! Looking good. I guess your mom's got a bum wheel."

Mom held her arms and screamed when she saw him, and he went over and picked her up out of her seat. I got him a cold beer from the fridge.

"Okay, Collin," my Mom said. "It's time for you to go to bed."

"Ah, c'mon," Clyde said. "Let the little guy hang out awhile."

"You like him?" Mom said and giggled.

"Sure, he's a funny guy."

"He is funny. Oh, you have to see him dance. Honey, put on 'ABC.'"

"ABC. You always get As in school, don't you?" Clyde said and winked at me. I didn't know what to say. I got Bs mostly and Cs sometimes.

"I'm just messing with you," he said.

I put the record on and danced like I remembered the Jackson 5 dancing on *The Ed Sullivan Show*. They laughed.

I had another beer, and Clyde told stories about being out at sea, fishing for crab. Then he took out a baggie, and Mom said it was really time for me to go to bed. I went upstairs to my room and laid in bed, but they were loud. I felt really thirsty all of a sudden but couldn't go down for water.

The laughing got closer, and I heard a heavy foot on the stairs. I got out of bed and crept out into the hallway. I peeked down the stairs, and Clyde was carrying Mom. She was giggling, and he seemed wobbly. I was worried he'd fall and drop her. I went back to my room and listened to make sure they made it. They went to her room and started making noises like the last time he came over. I couldn't take it and went downstairs. I drank three glasses of water from the kitchen and fell asleep on the couch.

* * *

They woke me up in the morning, talking in the kitchen. I pretended to still be asleep, and they didn't notice me at first. When they did, they started whispering. Clyde said something about his mom and medication, and I peeked through my eyelids. The envelope was in Mom's hand, and Clyde gave her a big hug and kiss.

Mom nudged me after he left. "How'd you end up down here?"

"You guys were being loud."

"I know. Sorry about that. Your mom gets lonely sometimes. Lemme make you breakfast."

She made bacon and eggs and toast and talked about a recent Bigfoot sighting only an hour away.

"Did they get it on film?"

"No, I don't think so. They were hunting."

"What if it was a bear?"

She ashed her cigarette. "Now who could mistake a bear for Bigfoot?"

When she got up to go to the bathroom, I ran to the counter and checked the envelope. There were still three hundred-dollar bills left.

I went over to Shelley's while her mom was at work, and we tried to get into the room that was locked. We tried to pry it open with one of her mom's records, but it was too thick. Shelley's school folder didn't work either. There was a hole in the doorknob where you put the key, and we looked in her mom's dresser drawers, careful to leave everything as it was. We couldn't find it, but Shelley said there was a screwdriver set in the garage. The smallest one just fit through, and we messed with it for a while until finally it clicked. We looked at each other. I pushed the door open and saw handlebars poking out over the bed.

"I see it!" I yelled.

Shelley screamed. We ran around the bed. It was a purple Huffy with a basket. She climbed on and rang the bell.

"Lemme try! Lemme try!" I said. We took turns getting off and on it. There were other presents sitting on the bed. I put on her new rain boots and tried to do the hula hoop, but it kept falling to the floor.

* * *

Mom's leg was getting better, and she was moving around easier. On the night of Christmas Eve, she stood up and said, "Look at me. Look at me." She lifted her good leg off the ground and balanced on her broken one. "I can put my weight on it." She leaned forward and held her arms out like a ballerina.

"Be careful," I started to say, but it was too late. She fell and yelped and I hurried over. She rolled onto her back and was laughing.

I went to bed early because I knew if I fell asleep early, the morning would get there faster, but that night I couldn't sleep. I listened for sounds like a bike being wheeled inside. I wondered where she could've hid it. I don't know if I slept at all.

When I first heard Mom downstairs in the morning, I jumped out of bed and ran down. I came into the kitchen and looked at the fireplace, but there was no bike, just a little box the size of a microwave. I thought maybe she had it somewhere else.

"Merry Christmas, Collin!" Mom said and gave me a hug. She pointed at the box with her crutch and raised her eyebrows. "Go on and open it."

I went and peeled off the tape and opened it up. It was full of packing peanuts, and I dug in there and pulled out something black. I held it up, confused—some kind of fancy goggles. I looked at Mom.

"Night vision goggles! New technology," she said. "You know they're nocturnal."

I made myself smile. "Neat," I said.

"Come on out to the garage." She got up and walked without her crutch. I got excited again. Maybe it was in there. I hurried behind her. She flicked on the light, but there was nothing.

"I got myself a pair too, so we can go together," she said. "I already got the batteries in it. Try them on." I put them on, and they weighed down my head.

"Hold on," she said and cut out the lights. Everything

was black except her body. It glowed orange, like something from the future. She growled and did a bumbling ape walk. She swatted at me.

"We're gonna find one, Mom," I said. "I know we will."

Tilikum Gets Loose

The walkway to the back entrance was narrow, with security guards at the partitions. I sprinted and shielded my face as the protesters threw rocks and called me a piece of shit. A bottle shattered at my feet. "Rot in hell, Bo!" one of them yelled. They recognized me and everyone else who worked at SeaWorld Tulsa. They'd been camped out outside the park for a month already, since the *Blackfish* documentary came out.

I unlocked the door and ducked inside and wiped the dust and beer off as best I could. The main entrance was closed off, so everyone came through the back, even the visitors, and they got shit thrown at them too. I walked down the stairs to the hallway with the thick glass walls of the tank. If you stood there, it wasn't long before the orca Tilikum would swim by and you'd tense up and stop breathing. The tank here was a lot smaller than the one in

Orlando.

Aaron Larson came down the hall. I said "What's up?" but he just walked past me in his wetsuit like I wasn't there. He had a chance of going to the Olympics for swimming and was a huge douchebag. The only trainers left were cocky and felt invincible. Aaron thought he could outswim the animals.

I climbed the three flights of stairs to the top of Shamu Stadium and unlocked the roll-up door of the ice cream shop. Most people had quit so I had to work solo. Mary would say I could get a shitty job anywhere, why did it have to be at SeaWorld? But that was my point. It was the best ice cream serving job in the world. I got to see Tilly every day. *Blackfish* had turned Mary against the place too.

I wiped the counter down and started the snowcone and soft serve machines. The park didn't open for another five minutes. I went back out to the concourse and wiped down the glass of the scuba suit display. It was from the thirties, and the helmet was made of brass. It came with the original Aqua-Lung. It was from one of the first deep dives made by man or something. I imagined going under with that thing on, trusting it with your life. It was like how the first people in space just had to trust that their spacesuits would hold up. People never stopped at the display. They just wanted to see Tilikum.

I walked to the back row of seats. Tilly was on the surface doing laps, ready for his first show of the day. When *Blackfish* came out, animal rights groups went nuts, and the feds ordered SeaWorld to stop breeding orcas. I think they moved Tilly here hoping people might forget about him. We were so happy because we'd never had an orca before.

42

SeaWorld didn't want to get rid of him because his sperm was too valuable. He made the biggest, most athletic whales. The documentary said that killer whales are really smart and hate being in captivity. Signs around the park said the SeaWorld orcas were healthier and happier than wild ones. I didn't know what to believe.

It was July and hot out, and people flooded in and bought ice cream in plastic orca bowls. A trainer got on the megaphone and started doing his spiel for the crowd. He said his name was Gary, and I didn't recognize him. Must've been his first show. I gave the last kid in line his snowcone and went out to watch.

Gary stood on the concrete shore, trying to get a clap going, but the crowd wasn't having it. Tilly swam around the tank and waved with one of his huge flippers. He came back to Gary, and Gary tossed some fish into his mouth.

Gary rode around on Tilly's back, and they both waved. The music picked up and they went under. Tilly launched him fifteen feet into the air, and he made a perfect dive back in, but the crowd still gave them nothing. They just fanned themselves with their cardboard orcas on a stick. Tilly shrieked at them. He was getting frustrated.

He didn't swim over to pick Gary up like he should've, and my stomach tightened. Gary headed back to the shore to reset. Tilly's fin dipped under the surface, and a second later he had Gary by the foot. He dragged him along the edge of the tank, showing him to the crowd. He was condemning them. It was like he was saying, "Isn't this what you wanted? Are you happy now?"

He took him under for twenty seconds or so then let go. Everyone stood out of their seats to watch, and people from the back rows ran down the steps to stand by the glass. Just before Gary would get to the nearest wall, Tilly'd grab him again and take him back under. He did this over and over, holding Gary down a little longer each time until he drowned. He could be so cruel sometimes.

* * *

The park closed at 8 p.m., and Mary picked me up in the F-150. When we got home she put *Blackfish* on in the den, and we started fixing tacos. She liked to have it on all the time in the background. I told her how Tilly did it again, and she said the trainers deserved whatever happened to them. "It's like when people get gored in the Running of the Bulls," she said. It was all just sad to me, for everybody. The trainers didn't know any better. Where else could kids get a chance to see an orca in real life? We started arguing about it again, but she got mad so fast.

We spread out on the sectional in the den to eat, and it was at the part where Tilly is a baby and gets torn from his mother off the coast of Iceland. In the wild, killer whales stay with their parents for life.

At 10 p.m., I asked if we could watch the news, and she shrugged. I turned it and there was Ashley Barnes, the main field reporter for NBC Tulsa. She was wearing a tight button-up, and her hair was in curls. She was gorgeous. She was standing on the shore of the river and pointing at the 23rd Street bridge. It was about a mile from our little house.

Ashley wrapped up and sent it back to the studio, and they played a video from a cop's dashcam. It showed an Audi A6 doing some crazy speed through downtown.

When it got to the bridge, it slowed down like the driver was giving up, but then it crawled over the short curb and through the rail and fell off the edge into the river. It was a big drop, and the cop in the car said, "Oh my lord!" They said the car sank, that the driver had drowned. A picture of a girl popped up on the screen with her name underneath, Cassie Wilkins. "Twenty-three years old," they said.

"Oh shit!" I said. Me and Mary looked at each other. I'd known Cassie since elementary school. She dropped out junior year and bought that Audi with her own money. I'd been buying from her since she started selling awful weed and her Adderall prescription in seventh grade. "She's dead," Mary said.

"What'd she do that for?" I said. "What the fuck?" She used to come by the house with the weed. Sometimes she'd come inside and smoke a bowl and shoot the shit with me. I hadn't heard much from her in the last few years since she started messing with bigger amounts. I never told Mary, but I think she knew. Cassie was the first person I had sex with.

"Are you okay?" Mary said.

"That's my buddy."

* * *

I wasn't asleep around 5 a.m. when someone tapped on our front door. Mary was a deep sleeper and didn't move. I laid still and felt scared, but the person wouldn't go away and kept tapping. I thought about waking Mary up but didn't want to annoy her.

I got out of bed and crept to the door. I looked through the peephole and saw the top of a head. It was a short person, and I felt less afraid. I opened the door, and she said, "Lemme in," and looked over her shoulder, back at the street. I was looking at a damn ghost. I'd forgotten how small Cassie was, the tiny boss. I stepped back to let her in. She was wearing sweatpants and a dirty white tank top. She was sunburned bad with a big gash on her forehead. I just stared at her, and she sat down on the couch.

"The TV said you died," I said.

She smiled. "I did but now I'm back." She acted like we'd just talked the day before. It'd been two years at least.

"Oh my God. I'm so glad you're alive."

"I'm dying of thirst, Bo," she said, and I went and got her water. She rubbed the gash on her forehead and said her head smacked the steering wheel when she hit the water.

"Oh my God," I said and asked if she needed ice, but she said she was fine. She'd slid out of the car window before it sank and hid under the bridge until the cop left. She just poked her mouth above the surface to breathe.

"That's crazy," I said. "I would've died for sure."

"Cops are lazy," she said. "I don't think he looked around." She found a spot to hide on the bank upriver. The cop came back later with the news crews, and Cassie stayed hidden on the shore all day.

Mary woke up while I was digging in her dresser for clothes. I told her what was going on. "This is a crime," she said. "It's called aiding and abetting."

"Aren't you happy she's alive?" I said. "Plus they think she's dead. They're not even gonna be looking for her."

I gave Cassie some clothes and my green towel. I told her she could crash for a night or two. She stretched out on the couch and closed her eyes.

46

Mary found the video of Cassie going off the bridge on the NBC Tulsa YouTube channel. We sat up in bed and watched it over and over. "She really should be dead," Mary said.

"Yeah, seriously. She shoulda been knocked out by the impact."

"Well, she's lucky she hit her forehead," Mary said. "It's the hardest part of the head." I wondered how she knew that. She knew everything. We wondered why she did it and figured she had a bunch of coke in the car or something.

"It's kinda genius when you think about it," I said. She avoided a felony and years in prison. The cops would never bother fishing the car out. They were too broke and stretched thin. The city had only gotten SeaWorld to come by agreeing to pay for the park.

* * *

Cassie was sitting on the couch when I got up in the morning. I asked if she wanted cereal or Pop-Tarts.

"Just coffee," she said. She looked worried.

"Are you gonna turn yourself in?" I said.

She looked at me like I was nuts. She patted the couch cushion next to her, and I went and sat down. "I gotta stay dead for now," she said.

"You owe somebody?"

"I gotta get to my car. You gotta help me."

"I wish I could but—" I started to say, but she cut me off.

"You work at SeaWorld still, right? Y'all have all kinds of equipment. Scuba gear."

"Yeah, I mean. I'm not a trainer. I could be one probably but—"

"Listen," she whispered. "There's fifty grand in that trunk, okay? I'll give you ten if you let me stay here and help me."

"Oh shit," I said. I kept my cool and said maybe, that I had to talk to Mary.

"But fucking no one else," she said.

"Of course not," I said and went to the bedroom. I closed the door behind me and shook Mary awake. "Cassie says there's fifty grand in the trunk of the Audi and that she'll give us ten if we help her get it and let her stay here."

She turned to me with her eyes still closed. "What?"

I told her again, and she opened her eyes and sat up. "What do you think?" I said, and she held up her hand. She needed to think. I left her there and went to take a shower. I had work.

When I got out, Mary was on her laptop. She was watching scuba diving instructional videos. "It'll be easy," she said. "You can just take the equipment from work."

"No. You don't understand," I said. "I work in the ice cream shop. I don't even know where that stuff is. They wouldn't let me anywhere near it."

"You gotta make some friends."

"I dunno," I said. "Plus the river current is strong. Someone would see us."

"It's not that strong," she said.

"But you're not really a swimmer."

"I can swim. I was on the Little Dolphins team when I was little, and the coach would tell the other kids to watch my form."

"Underwater though?"

"Yeah, I'll use that one stroke where you push your arms sideways. It's how you're supposed to swim underwater. I'm fit."

"Well, you're skinny."

She got worked up and decided she was gonna prove it to me. "Tomorrow at the river," she said. I had Thursdays off. Mary was between jobs. She'd have some cashier job for a little bit then cuss out the manager or something. She didn't have a degree, but she was college-educated. I couldn't imagine being as smart as her and have to take orders from some idiot.

She drove me to the park and had to let me out further away than usual. The crowd of protesters had grown. As I got closer, I realized there were two groups fighting with each other. No one noticed me, and I stood there and watched. One lady had a sign that said "Punishment Comes for Tilikum." I asked her what was going on, and she said that if orcas were so smart and aware, they should be held accountable for their actions.

"That makes sense," I said. It was kinda like what Mary was saying. They were just like us. Maybe it wasn't SeaWorld's fault. Maybe Tilly was just born bad, like Ted Bundy. I still loved him though. Who were we to judge him? None of us had been through what he had. None of us knew what it was like to be stuck in a pool when everything inside tells you you should be roaming the oceans. I doubted he could make it out there, though.

The security guards were gone, replaced by state troopers. They had the two groups on opposite sides of the partitioned walkway. I told one of the cops that I worked here, and he escorted me to the door.

My shift went smooth until the last show. There was screaming, and the customers in line ran to go see. I followed them. I found an empty seat in the back row and stood on it. Tilikum had Aaron Larson in his mouth. Aaron screamed and flailed his arms. Just his torso hung out, and red streaked behind them.

After it was over, Tilly kept playing with the body. He tore the limbs off one at a time and flung them into the stands. People lost interest and had started filing out when it happened. An explosion went off. There was a huge blast and the sound of glass shattering, and then I couldn't hear anything. The ground shook, and I was thrown onto the people in front of me. We were piled together, and we clawed at each other to get away. I made it out and crawled back towards the ice cream shop. I used the counter to pull myself up and laid on it and tried to roll inside, but someone grabbed me and dragged me back to the concrete ground. The guy had me by the collar and was yelling something. He looked at me the way the protesters did, and then he kicked me in the face.

I was laying on my side when I came to. One of my eyes was closed shut. I touched my face, a mess of blood. I could hear again—screaming and yelling, but I didn't see anyone around me. Smoke was everywhere.

I got to my feet and saw that the other side of the stadium was on fire. The only way out was down the stadium stairs, but the smoke pushed me back down the concourse. It stung my eyes and burned my throat. I leaned against the wall and felt glass. The ancient scuba suit display was still unbroken.

I closed my eyes and held my breath as best I could and went to the ice cream counter. I rolled my body back inside and felt for the snowcone machine. I ripped the cord out of the socket and carried it back over the counter. The smoke was getting even thicker. I stumbled to the display and put the machine on my shoulder and heaved it at the scuba gear. I hardly heard the glass shatter from all the noise. I reached in and cut myself on a jagged shard and pulled out the Aqua-Lung. I put it on like a backpack and took the helmet off its mount and put it on. It was heavy, but suddenly I could breathe again and open my eyes. I headed down the stadium stairs, dragging the suit behind me.

Through the little barred helmet window, I couldn't see Tilly in the water. I went down to the tank glass but still didn't see him anywhere. The fire was spreading to my side. There was no time. I turned around and rushed down the stairwell and out the building. The partitions were knocked over, and the state troopers were gone. I set the helmet down and tore off my work shirt so people wouldn't recognize me. I checked my phone, and there were 23 missed calls from Mary. I put the helmet back on and hurried toward where she would usually pick me up. People screamed and rocks rang against the helmet. I saw the F-150. My Mary. She'd come for me. I took off the helmet and ran to her. She reached over and pushed the door open. I threw the scuba stuff in the bed and got in. Her eyes were huge.

"What the hell is that?"

"That really old scuba suit I told you about, with the original Jacques Cousteau Aqua-Lung. Remember?"

"Whatever. What about Tilly?" she said.

"I don't know. I couldn't see him."

* * *

I iced down my face while we sat on the sectional and watched the news for updates. Ashley reported live from SeaWorld. The rioters were gone, the park was mostly reduced to ashes. Ashley said it was definitely a bomb someone put by the tank. Around midnight, she confirmed that Tilikum was dead. He swam through the glass wall where the bomb went off. A shot from a helicopter showed his huge body laid out on the concrete.

We went to bed, and Mary sank under the covers and started crying. Once she started, it came out of me too. We held each other, and it sank in that I'd never see him again. I'd never stand at the glass wall again while he swam by. I got tissues for us from the bathroom and took deep breaths. I started to feel almost relieved. Tilly had been so sick, and finally, he had peace, the peace he'd wanted ever since he was a calf and they took him from his mom. That's what I kept telling Mary, but she just kept crying, and I held her until she fell asleep.

I was still wide awake, and I heard the TV on in the living room. I slid out from under Mary and found Cassie smoking a bowl on the couch. "Oh my God," she said when she saw my face. She got up and came up to me. "I heard about everything. I'm so glad you made it out." She went to touch my cheek, but I pushed her hand away. "Someone hit you?"

"Kicked me."

She frowned. "Ouch. You need a bowl. That's what you need. Sit down." She loaded the pipe and let me have greens. I sank into the couch, and Cassie flipped through the channels. We stumbled on an infomercial for this thing called the Potty Putter.

"What the fuck?" Cassie said. It was this tiny putting green you put in front of your toilet so you could practice golf while you took a shit. It came with a little putter club. The people looked fucking ridiculous, and we couldn't stop laughing.

Tired of reading the same boring newspaper while on the toilet? Try working on that short game!

"Imagine if someone couldn't make it and had like a meltdown," Cassie said. She sat on the edge of the couch like she was on the toilet. She threw her hands in the air and stomped her feet.

"Stop! Stop it!" I said, howling.

For that little bit, I wasn't thinking about Tilly at all.

* * *

Thousands showed up to the ruins of the water park to honor Tilly and all the fallen animals. We lit each other's white candles, and me and Mary both cried. Someone made a huge black wreath shaped like Tilly's fin—folded over. It happened to all captive males but almost never in the wild. There were lots of different theories why, like maybe because captive whales spend a lot more time at the surface and eventually gravity brings the fins down. Mary said it showed the collapse of their spirits.

We held our candles in the air while a guy on a megaphone said Tilly's death wouldn't be in vain. I heard a shrill cry come from behind us. It made me shiver, but no one else's head moved. I couldn't ask her if she heard it too.

* * *

The next morning, I told Mary how I was worried about money. With SeaWorld gone, we had nothing coming in.

"We're gonna get that briefcase, remember?" she said. She talked about her scuba diving plan again. "Only slight issue is getting the equipment."

"Can't we just rent it?" I said.

"You gotta be certified."

"How hard is it to get certified?"

"I already looked at it. It's expensive," she said and got her laptop out. "Five hundred bucks at this one place, and that doesn't include equipment rental."

"Christ."

"This one place lets you try a class for free," she said, then gave me this look. She had an idea. "I'll go to the free class under a fake name and run off with the equipment when the moment is right."

I thought about it. It might work. "I don't think you're a good enough swimmer," I said and smiled. She slapped my thigh.

"I am too!"

"Prove it."

She changed into a swimsuit, and we took the F-150 to the river. I dipped my hand in the water and stopped myself from laughing. It was freezing, but no way Mary was gonna back down. She got in and tried to hide her shivering. She went under and came back up right away, gasping. "I can't hold my breath. The water's so cold," she said. "My body needs a second. To get acclimated. When I have a wetsuit on, it'll be a non-factor."

54

She tried again but got pushed downstream. "Agh," she cried. "My foot touched something." She kicked back and splashed, and I figured she was just stalling. "What the fuck? What the fuck is that?" she said and clawed at the grass on the shore, and I helped her out. She was actually scared.

"What?"

"I dunno. I think there's a leg." She pointed by the tree roots. I got closer and pulled the bush back and jumped. There was a man's leg, hairy and pale, not attached to a body. I swear to God, right then, I heard a high-pitched cry, the same one from the vigil. I froze up and felt faint and just caught myself before I fell in the water. I crouched down and peeled the leaves back.

"I found an arm," Mary said. She'd gone ten yards upriver.

"This is a murder," I said.

"Definitely homicide."

We'd finally stumbled on a corpse. It had only been a matter of time. We knew from documentaries on the ID channel that bodies were everywhere. "Not his first time," I said. "He's bored with regular murder." There's a lot you can tell about a killer from the crime scene.

"Probably a loner," Mary said. She called 911, and it took half an hour for a cop to show up. I tried to tell her about our loner theory, but she wasn't interested. She seemed exhausted and fed up. The protests at SeaWorld were more than Tulsa PD could handle. A detective came, and they separated me and Mary, and I answered how she'd told me to. We came to the river just to get our feet wet. Soon there were a bunch of camera crews around the scene, in town from all over because of the SeaWorld stuff.

When Ashley Barnes from NBC Tulsa came, everyone made a path for her. She wanted to interview me. Her perfume was strong, and she was even more beautiful in person. I had to tell her to give me a second because I was starstruck, and she laughed and told me I didn't have to be nervous around her. If only she knew how many times I'd jerked off to her on the TV when Mary was out of the house. If only she knew what we were really up to.

* * *

It was crazy, seeing myself on TV with Ashley. Mary laughed at me and said I sounded nervous. Cassie wasn't laughing though. She stood up from the sectional and folded her arms.

"Are you okay?" I said.

She shook her head. "How are we gonna get to the car now? What if they pull the car out looking for evidence?"

She was paranoid and didn't know how things worked. She didn't watch the ID channel.

"Don't worry," Mary said. "They're probably already gone. Probably collected all the evidence. Even if they're there, I'll just get in downriver and slide in right under their noses."

"When?"

"My first scuba lesson is tomorrow. I should be able to get the stuff."

"Yeah, here, this is just worrying you," I said. "Lemme turn it off and put on *Blackfish*."

"No!" Cassie said. "I don't wanna watch *Blackfish*. I'm

so sick of that goddamn documentary."

Mary's eyes lit up. "Listen. While you're staying in our house, you can either watch what we watch and keep your mouth shut or you can leave." She pointed at the front door. Cassie looked at me, but I looked away. She got up and went to the spare bedroom. I'd made a pallet for her and told her she could smoke in there if she opened the window.

Me and Mary put on the doc, and this scientist talked about how smart Tilly was. Mary had taught me that killer whales are actually dolphins, not whales. Everyone knows dolphins are really smart, and orcas are the smartest kind of dolphin. Mary said they're so smart there can be good ones and bad ones and disturbed-but-still-good ones.

Blackfish said that Tilly was deeply traumatized. After they captured him from the sea, they put him in a tiny tank with two adult females at this park in Canada called Sealand. The females bullied him constantly and raked his skin open with their teeth. He kept trying to kill himself by ramming his head into the walls, but the pool wasn't long enough for him to build up enough speed.

* * *

After Mary went to bed, I went to check on Cassie. Her light was still on, but she didn't answer when I knocked. I opened the door and she wasn't there. The window was a few inches open.

I waited for her on the couch. It was quiet besides the cicadas. After a while, there were the same sharp cries I heard before, off in the distance, and I felt like I was back at the river. I wondered if it was Tilly, calling to me from the other side.

It was past 2 a.m. when I heard Cassie come back through the window. I knocked soft, and she let me in.

"I just wanted to check on you after, ya know, with Mary."

She waved her hand. "No worries."

"Okay, good. Where'd you go?"

"I'll show you," she said and smiled. She pulled an eight-ball of coke out of her pocket, and I got excited like you do when drugs just show up. I remembered junior year, doing lines with her off Eddie Cox's bathroom sink.

We needed something to chop it up on. I slipped out of the room and got Mary's hand mirror. I grabbed the Keystone Light six-pack from the fridge. We took bumps and washed them down with the beer. We rubbed it in our gums and couldn't feel our mouths and lips. We talked about that time Taylor Ruggs was stumbling around drunk and fell through her parents' glass coffee table.

"It's been great seeing you again," I said.

She smiled like she hadn't since she got here. "Yeah. It's been great seeing you too." We were sitting cross-legged with our knees touching, the mirror sitting between us.

"For the longest time, it was you and me."

"Yeah," she said. She was looking right back at me. She leaned in and I could tell we were gonna kiss, but it's hard to stop once it's right there. We kissed but didn't feel it.

We leaned back away from each other. I asked her how much weight she had sold for the money in the Audi that night. She shook her head.

"None. I haven't sold a gram in months," she said.

"What? But all that money?"

She looked down. "I gotta tell you something," she said. "But you can't tell Mary, okay?" I nodded, and she said, "It's not money in the briefcase."

"What? Really?"

She shook her head. "It's Tilikum's semen," she said and smiled.

"Are you serious?"

She nodded.

"What the fuck? Why?"

"I was working with SeaWorld. They're still breeding orcas in secret. Isn't that wild?"

"Crazy. Yeah." She'd lied to me. "You lied."

"I know. I'm sorry," she said and put her face in her hands. "I feel bad, but I had to tell you something. I'm so scared."

"Listen, we can't help you anymore," I said and stood up.

She got up and grabbed my arm with both hands. "Bo, you gotta. I'm dead if I don't get that briefcase."

"Just get out of Tulsa. They'll never find you. Everyone thinks you're dead."

"You don't understand. It's not some drug dealer who's after me. It's SeaWorld. The last of his semen is in that car. You don't know what it's worth. They're worse than the cops. If I show my face anywhere and I don't have it—"

I didn't know what to say. I couldn't take her looking at me with those eyes. "If you don't help me, I'm dead," she said. Damn. It was fucking Cassie Wilkins from way back.

"Okay, okay," I said. "I'll try."

* * *

The next morning, another body with the limbs torn off was found near the bridge. Police Chief Proctor gave a big press conference on NBC Tulsa announcing there was a serial killer on the loose. Proctor was a dusty old man with a gray mustache. He talked about all the details. He said the limbs seemed crudely torn off instead of cut or sawed off. The puncture wounds were wide and round, so it probably wasn't a knife. Then the detectives did side interviews with Ashley Barnes. They were loving the attention.

"They're gonna drag everything out of that river, I bet," Cassie said.

"That's what Tilly would do to the trainers," I said.

"What?" Mary said.

"Tear them apart."

"This doesn't sound like a man," Mary said.

Cassie laughed.

"What Proctor said sounds like bite marks. Big bite marks," I said. I looked at Mary. "Could it be him somehow? Tilikum?"

"Well, do you believe in ghosts, ghosts of humans?" she asked.

"I don't know. Maybe."

"Alright," Cassie said. "This is officially too fucking ridiculous for me." She went out to the backyard to smoke.

Mary was thinking. "Well, orcas are just as conscious and emotionally developed as we are, and I think it's our consciousness that makes people think humans have souls or spirits or whatever, which I think is what most people think ghosts are—souls that live on after the body dies."

"Yeah. Why would he do this?"

"Maybe his spirit is still restless. He's still angry."

I wanted to tell her about the cries I'd been hearing, how it felt like he was calling for me. Maybe I was next. "Do you think Tilly is bad?"

Mary smiled and shrugged. "Who can say?"

* * *

Mary came back from scuba class without any gear. "We just did these breathing exercises and swam around and shit," she said. "The guy didn't even take the stuff out. I'll get it soon though. Don't worry." She went to the bedroom and motioned with her eyes for me to follow her. She went and closed the door and whispered, "We're fucked."

"What? Why?"

"There's not gonna be another class. They make you pay before the second class." She sat on the bed, and I sat next to her. "What if we waited for one of the workers to walk to their car then took their keys?"

"Like mug them?" I said.

"No, no. Just like push them down and take their keys. We wouldn't hit them or take their wallet or anything."

"We can't do that," I said. "Plus then they'll know someone has keys to the building."

"Yeah. Why's it so hard to get goddamn scuba stuff? I wonder if I could just hold my breath."

"Stop," I said. "It's a deep dive." Deep dive. A real journey into the murky waters like the pioneers did. I thought about the ancient scuba suit sitting in the hallway closet—made of real materials, brass and rubber, before all this synthetic shit came around. The fire had pushed me to it for a reason. Tilly was calling me to the river. I had to face

61

him. "We're going tonight," I said and stood up.

"What?"

I went out to the hallway and got the gear out of the closet. I dragged it to the back porch. "We're going tonight," I told Cassie. Mary followed me outside. I laid everything out.

"What are you doing?" Mary said.

"We got a scuba suit right here."

"You're not serious," she said and put her hands on her hips. "I'm not going in that thing."

"I know. It wouldn't fit you. I'm gonna do it."

"No way. You're not a swimmer."

"Yes, I am. I worked at a water park."

"Serving ice cream."

I stepped into the heavy rubber suit. "Yeah but I think eventually I would've worked my way up to trainer. Maybe with the porpoises, and the belugas."

"Belugas? Fine. Whatever."

I put my arms in, and it fit me well. I knew it had to be me. Mary told me not to work at SeaWorld, but I couldn't stay away.

We took turns blowing air into the Aqua-Lung, but my chest felt tight, and it was hard to muster anything. Right then, there was a shrill cry in the distance. I felt dizzy.

"Are you okay?" Mary said.

"Yeah, I'm just gonna try on the helmet." I picked up the heavy bronze thing and set it on my head. I could barely see through the tiny barred window.

"This shit makes no sense," Mary said and threw down the Aqua-Lung. "This can't be how you fill up an air tank."

I felt my legs give out, and I barely got my arms back to

catch myself. I hit the ground and felt like I couldn't breathe. Mary got the helmet off. "Oh God, Bo. Did you faint?"

"Kinda," I said, huffing and puffing.

"You're gonna fucking drown in this thing," Mary said, her voice cracking. "It's not a scuba suit. It's a coffin. We don't know what we're doing." She sniffled. "I don't care about the fucking money. I'll get a shitty job."

She cared about me. "But Tilly. He wants me," I said and sat up. "He's calling me."

"What?"

"I've been hearing these orca cries, and something is pulling me to the river. It's hard to describe. It's because I worked there."

Mary stared into the sky and shook her head. "You wanna end up like that guy we found? Torn to pieces?"

Tears came up. She loved me. I stood up and helped her up and squeezed her tight. "I don't wanna die," I said and bawled like a baby.

"No. What good would that do?" she said and rubbed my back. "Tilikum!" she yelled at the sky. "If you can hear me, please listen. I hope that one day you find peace in death. Forgive me for going to SeaWorld when I was three. It wasn't my choice, and I didn't understand what was going on. Please forgive my boyfriend, Bo."

"I just wanted to be near you," I said, sobbing.

"He just wanted to be near you, Tilly. Ask yourself, will killing one more person make you feel better? I mean, where does it all end?"

We stood there in silence. Another cry came, louder this time, and I grimaced. "I just sold ice cream."

"Yeah, you were just a pawn. You, the trainers. Y'all

didn't put him in that tank."

"No."

"That's why he's not satisfied," Mary said, her eyes lighting up. "He's not getting vengeance on the right people, the higher-ups, the masterminds."

The back door opened and Cassie poked her head out. "What are y'all yelling about?"

"Nothing. Go back inside," Mary said, and Cassie slammed the sliding door hard.

"Why are you so mean to her?"

"She's a snake in the grass."

"Yeah," I said. "I gotta tell you something."

I told her everything.

* * *

We decided we'd go at midnight when it was darkest. It took forever to get here. Cassie stayed in her room, and I could smell her chain smoking. Me and Mary watched Blackfish on a loop in Tilly's honor. I felt wired and couldn't eat dinner. I couldn't sit still. The cries came more often. He was mad, hungry.

At 11:30 p.m., we figured it was dark enough. I knocked on Cassie's door, and she looked like shit. She obviously hadn't showered or slept in a while. We loaded the scuba stuff in the truck and headed for the river. Tilly's screams stung more the closer we got but went quiet when we parked on the bank. We got out, and I carried everything to the shore. The three of us stood there, the water licking our feet. The cries came back so sharp I grimaced and covered my ears.

"What?" Cassie said.

"Nothing. I got this killer headache." I started to put on the rubber suit. Cassie handed me the Aqua-Lung, and I slung it across my back, connected the front straps.

Glaring in the moonlight, I saw a folded-over fin in the river. He wanted me, and there I was. Mary was saying something.

"Oh, we forgot that thing in the car."

"Huh?" I said. The fin was moving with the stream towards us. My feet felt stuck in the mud.

"The connector hose thing. Where'd you put it? Show me." Mary took my arm and pulled me away. "Cassie, can you rinse off the helmet window? It's dirty."

Cassie bent down to the water, and I saw the fin disappear under the surface. Mary pulled me, hard this time, until I turned towards the truck. We took a few steps up the shore, and air rushed past us. There was a big splash and no time for a scream.

Soon the water was calm again, and it was quiet besides the cicadas. We stayed on the shore for a while, in the truck, her head on my shoulder. When we got back to the house, there was no way we were gonna sleep. We sat on the couch but didn't put the TV on.

Monticello

Dessie came in first from recess and woke up Ms. Clemson. She smiled and got her eyelids half-open and asked where they were in social studies. "War of 1812," Dessie said, and the bell rang, and the rest of the class hurried in, sweaty.

Ms. Clemson slurred through the lesson. "What can anyone tell me about the second war with the British?"

Cory Starks shook his head and looked around the classroom. "It was about trade with France," he said.

"Yes, certainly," Ms. Clemson said, leaning against the chalkboard.

It went quiet before Dessie jumped in. "Andrew Jackson beat the British in the Battle of New Orleans even though the treaty had already been signed. They didn't get the news in time. They didn't have phones back then. Jackson was president later on."

"Perfect, Desmond. Yes, Andrew was a president of this United States."

Dessie carried her until the final bell went off at 3:30 and stayed with her in 107. He took out his math book and found some long division exercises to do. "You forgot to give out homework again," he said.

"Did I? Damnit," she said. She circled the classroom, constantly checking the clock.

By four, the bus had left, and no more kids were waiting for their parents to pick them up. Dessie and Ms. Clemson packed up and headed to the teachers' lounge where they were all crowded around Dessie's desk. They whined and fought to get to the front, and Dessie waited in the doorway until they formed a line. Dad always said that people use their habit as an excuse to devolve back to savage ways. He said that the difference between being a user and being a junkie was all about how you carry yourself.

Dessie took his seat, and old Mr. Lisicky held out a ten. He taught kindergarten in 108, next door to Ms. Clemson, and sometimes they could overhear him snoring through the wall. He'd been at Westington Elementary since it opened.

"Oxys are fifteen," Dessie said. He was running low. Dad had been lazy about making his rounds to the doctors for scripts.

"Ah, Dessie, c'mon. Are they gonna be twenty tomorrow?"

Dessie looked to Ms. Clemson standing next to him. "You know Desmond doesn't negotiate," she said. Mr. Lisicky dug another five from his pocket and gave her a dirty look. The music teacher, Mrs. Daughtry, got her little Vicodins. The State of Virginia was always talking about cutting the arts from the budget, and she was very worried. The other teachers got what they needed and shuffled off.

Ms. Clemson's Kia was the last car left in the parking lot. On the ride home, she asked Dessie why his dad hadn't been sleeping with her lately.

"Goddamnit, I don't know," he said. "He doesn't talk to me about any of that."

When they went through the front door, it was quiet. Usually, Dad came up to Dessie right away, wanting to talk, after being alone all day. They walked into the living room, and Dad was on the couch with a needle stuck in his arm. His face was too white.

He'd actually done it. The idiot.

Dessie ran out the front door and shed his backpack on the ground. Ms. Clemson called for him. He ran past mailboxes and past the busted cars lining the street. He ran out of breath and started walking. He heard Ms. Clemson's steps coming. He didn't want her to catch him and to have to hear her crying. He didn't want to go back into the house. He didn't want to keep moving. He collapsed in the yard of an abandoned house.

Ms. Clemson's cries were right behind him. He turned onto his back and kicked his legs out at her. "He promised he wouldn't!"

She knelt down in the grass. "No, no. He had a problem. It was an accident," she said through snot and tears.

"No," he said. "You don't know him. Dad didn't believe in overdoses."

She sat cross-legged next to him for a while in silence. He wondered if Dad had been warning him in a way—all the weird shit he'd been saying. He said when you shoot dope, you experience the bliss of death for a little, and it helps you transition into the real thing. They'd been eating microwave mac and cheese last week when he said the distinction between life and death was arbitrary.

Ms. Clemson stood up and held out her hands for Dessie. They walked slowly back to the house, and she kept her hand around his neck. They went inside, and she took out her cell phone.

"Who are you calling?" he said. "Don't call the cops."

"I have to, Desmond."

He swatted at the phone. "Don't! They'll put me in some group home."

She sighed and put it away.

"I just have to think," he said and walked toward the living room. She grabbed his shoulder, but he shook her off.

Dad looked hollow, like he weighed nothing. Whenever Dessie thought of him, he thought of him as strong and rough, even though he'd been shrinking for years. Ms. Clemson took the recliner and turned it away from Dad. She sat and did some kind of breathing exercise. Dessie lit a candle and looked at the pipe collection on the mantel. He'd never been allowed to touch the one in the glass case. It was from early nineteenth-century Hong Kong and made of bone.

He got a chair from the kitchen and dragged it into the living room. He set it under the mantel and stepped onto it. He got on his tippy-toes and just reached the glass top. He lifted it off and took the pipe from its holder. There was a little opium left in the jar. He hopped down and sat on the floor.

It crumbled like dry peanut butter, and he fixed it in the pipe and held it over the candle and let it cook. He stood up and handed the pipe to Ms. Clemson. She took a pull and sank into the recliner, and he breathed in her exhale.

* * *

Ms. Clemson was crying again when Dessie woke up in Dad's stiff lap. He'd crawled into it at some point, and he was crying too. He'd started in his sleep.

"We can't just leave him on the couch," she said.

Dad was dope-skinny but tall with broad shoulders, and it took everything they had to drag him to the master bedroom and get him onto his bed. Ms. Clemson kneeled on the carpet with her hands clasped, and Dessie yanked her arm. "Don't pray. He doesn't want that. He hates all that stuff."

They waited until dark to take him outside. The backyard was filled with poppy plants hidden in the uncut grass. The red flowers had blossomed and would fall out soon—almost time to harvest. Dessie cleared the corner by the fence and watched Ms. Clemson dig and told her all the things Dad had been saying about death, that he talked about Mom for the first time in forever, about how he'd see her again one day. "But I thought he didn't believe in an afterlife like that," Ms. Clemson said.

"I know," Dessie said. "But yeah. Sometimes he did."

* * *

Principal Felder made a show of pulling Dessie out of class during mandatory silent reading time. They did this dance every couple weeks when the teachers who weren't down complained about something. They didn't like how he used the teachers' lounge bathroom and skipped to the front of the lunch line.

Felder didn't use, but she was all about money. She got a cut, and it made everything easier. She wore gold earrings and necklaces and was proud of being principal.

On the way to her office, she tilted Dessie's chin up. "What's up with you today? You're quiet."

He shrugged. My dad is dead, he thought.

"Look like you could use a shower," she said. They went in her office, and she closed the door. "Dessie. We're *On Fire* again," she said. It was the worst possible grade and meant Westington could get shut down at any time.

"Goddamnit. But we just got put out. We just got off fire."

"I know, but we're back on. There've been complaints to the school board by parents—well, one parent, mostly—about the teachers. Falling asleep in class, not making sense. Last week Mr. Lisicky fell asleep on the toilet during lunch and was missing for the rest of the day."

"He's really old."

"His kids were wadding up pages from the picture books and throwing them at each other. We don't have money for new books. Well, I'm not paying for them, anyway."

The school lost students every week. Parents who could afford it were moving out of Westington or sending their kids to one of the private schools in downtown Richmond.

Dad had always said public education was a total failure like every other socialist idea, and he'd homeschooled Dessie until he just couldn't anymore. They'd do an hour of math in the morning then history and government until lunch. They didn't use books or anything. Dad just went off memory. Dessie knew from him that most history taught in public schools was bullshit.

"Whose parent complained?"

She didn't say anything, but she gave him this look saying it was exactly who he thought—Cory Starks' mom. Cory sat in Dessie's row, two seats ahead. Sometimes he got frustrated with Ms. Clemson's lessons. Ms. Starks put so much pressure on him, and all the teachers were scared of her.

* * *

Dessie sat on the bench in front of the swings drinking coffee from the teachers' lounge. He found that a cup really helped him get through the after-lunch drowsiness. Past the four-square courts and girls playing hopscotch, Mark Pataki and Bryan Rice played one-on-one basketball next to the jungle gym. They were overgrown fifth graders hit too soon by puberty. A Snack Pack of pudding each was all it took.

Cory was in the field behind the swings playing football. He played all-time quarterback because he had a cannon for an arm. Dessie got up and made his way to the jungle gym. He nodded at Mark and Bryan, and they started toward the field. Mrs. Lambert was the only monitor on duty. Just had to divert her. Dessie waited until Mark and Bryan were close to Cory, and he got on the monkey bars and swung to the middle and then dropped to the ground. He grabbed his ankle and screamed out in pain. He screamed as loud as he could, and kids surrounded him. "Are you okay?" they asked. Some ran for Mrs. Lambert, and soon she was kneeling by Dessie. He cried more.

"My ankle! My ankle!"

"Poor thing," she said. She's a good lady, he thought. Deserved to be at a better school. He tried to see what was going on in the field, but there were too many people in the way.

"Let's get you to the nurse. Do you think you can walk?"

"I dunno. I can try." She helped him up.

What he saw in the field wasn't right. Mark and Bryan were backpedaling. Cory walked at them with half the school behind him. He threw the football at Mark and Bryan, and the whole group charged the two bullies. Mark and Bryan ran to the asphalt playground and yelled for Mrs. Lambert. She blew her whistle, still helping Dessie walk, and everyone stopped. "What's going on here?"

Mark pointed at all the kids. "They were..." he said, out of breath. "We were playing."

Mrs. Lambert checked her watch. "We might as well go in now anyway. Line up."

The kids lined up by their classes.

"I'm okay. I can walk," Dessie said.

"Okay, but straight to the nurse when we get inside."

He limped to his line, and they went inside one row at a time. He looked up and saw Cory at the front of the line looking back at him with a dead-eye stare. It was their row's turn, and someone had to tap Cory to snap him out of it.

They went down the wide hallway to the classrooms, and Dessie broke off toward the nurse's office but walked past it and went to Felder's. She was blowing gum bubbles, and he told her what happened.

"I knew he was popular but not like this," he said. "He could turn the whole school against me."

She threw her hands up in surrender. "I can't even think about this shit right now. The assistant superintendent is coming next week for some inspection."

"Can't you see how it's all connected? Cory looked like a hero out there today. He's gonna be in everyone's ear about what's going on, and everyone is gonna complain to their parents. Suddenly, we'll have a hundred Ms. Starks nagging the school board."

She closed her eyes and shook her head. "It might be time to start thinking about your next move."

"I know. I know. I've just got to find a way to—"

"No, I mean like a new school, Dessie. A new city, even. You ever talk to your dad about it?"

He didn't answer right away.

"No," he said. "Never."

* * *

The faculty tried to stay sober the morning the assistant superintendent was supposed to come, but by 10:30 he still hadn't shown up. Ms. Clemson farted loud during math and ran out of the classroom. The class went wild, laughing and making fart sounds with their hands and mouths and armpits.

Dessie knew it was withdrawal coming on. There was

only one toilet in the lounge, so the teachers started using the kids' bathrooms. The stink went all the way down the hall, and Felder had to call a recess and open all the windows to let the building air out.

Dad said the keys were to never quit and never run out of money. That's when all the problems happened. He always said that opiates aren't inherently dangerous, and when people overdose on heroin it's because they quit for a while and then go right back to the amount they were using before. That, or they take something cut with some kind of poison, or that black tar shit. He loved to say, "Most people don't overdose on heroin. They overdose on poison."

Dessie and Felder stood at the lobby windows, looking out for the ASI. "I think he's doing it on purpose," Dessie said. "Like when CPS shows up a day early to catch parents off guard."

"Yeah, maybe."

The teachers were huddled out back by the swings, and Dessie went out and gave them what they needed. He told them to only take a little, just enough to get rid of the withdrawal, but of course they didn't listen, and by lunch, they were drooling.

Felder got bored of waiting and went back to her office and had Dessie stand watch. Around two, the assistant superintendent pulled into the parking lot in a little beat-up Toyota, and Dessie ran back to sound the alarm. The art teacher Mrs. Daughtry was jabbing her leg with scissors to stay awake, and Mr. Lisicky was hopeless in 108. He'd fallen out of his chair, and the six-year-olds had glued strips of construction paper to him and sprinkled him with glitter. Dessie shooed them away and checked Mr. Lisicky's pulse to make sure he was alive. He cut the lights and told the little ones not to make a sound or else. Threats were all they understood.

Dessie heard Felder down the hall talking to the ASI in her professional voice, and he went to 107 and got Ms. Clemson sitting up and talking sense. Everyone took out papers from their desks and tried to look busy. The voices got closer, and the kindergarteners next door burst out laughing and ruined everything.

Lisicky's door groaned as it opened. Dessie put his ear to the wall, and Felder made her fake chuckle. She tried to explain, something about narcolepsy and nondiscrimination. They grunted, trying to pick Mr. Lisicky up. Dessie knew this would probably happen. He slipped out of the classroom and hurried down the hall. He went out the back double doors and ran around the building with pills rattling in his pocket. They were OxyContins in a Vicodin prescription bottle. The word "OxyContin" scared folks. The news talked about people dying from it every day, but everyone liked Vicodin. Everyone'd had it at some point—after they got their wisdom teeth pulled or fell off their bike and broke something. Dad said that Big Pharma and the FDA made sure to get opioids in your bloodstream young.

Dessie set the bottle in the grass a few feet from the beat-up Toyota. Fifteen tabs. He'd thought a lot about the number. Fifteen was just enough so that someone could start popping them and think they'd never run out.

He hurried back to the side of the building and waited. The bright orange bottle really stuck out in the grass. The front doors opened and Felder thanked the ASI for coming out to Westington, and he assured her he'd be in contact soon. He walked to the Toyota with his gaze down, and from behind Dessie could tell he was young. He was short and chunky. Probably overworked and probably didn't have a girlfriend.

He paused a split second when he spotted the bottle and thought he was being slick by kicking it closer to his car. Dessie giggled. The ASI got in the Toyota and started the engine before leaning over and grabbing it and taking off.

* * *

That night, Ms. Clemson fixed Dessie's favorite again, mac and cheese with hot dog chunks. They ate in front of Thomas Jefferson, a reproduction of that portrait you always saw in books.

"Dad took me to Monticello a few months ago. You ever been?"

"A long time ago. When I was a girl, on a field trip."

"There was a tour guide, but we left the group because Dad knew more than him. Did you know Jefferson built the house with his bare hands?"

"Oh, wow."

"Did you know he grew poppies there?"

"Really?"

"Yeah, he was a dragon chaser. Can't really say it affected his work ethic."

"No."

He put his fork down. He didn't have much of an appetite. "Dad always told me Virginia was the birthplace of America, but all the power and wealth was stolen and moved up north to New York. He always told me, 'I am an American king and you're an American prince, Desmond.' He'd get in arguments with himself about it. Like, I'd hear him in his room go, 'And don't say anything about Washington, D.C. I'm talking about Rich-mond, Ver-gin-ya, where Patrick Henry said what he said, where Cornwallis surrendered.'" He laughed. "He wanted to name me Aaron at first, you know why?"

She shook her head. Her eyes were droopy.

"My mom didn't like the name and didn't know why Dad liked it so much, but then she figured it out. He wanted to name me after Aaron Burr, the guy who killed Hamilton."

"That's funny. Do you remember your mom?"

"No, but Dad talked about her sometimes."

Ms. Clemson's eyes closed, and she nodded, then she face-planted onto her mac and cheese. Dessie went over and shook her arm, but she didn't move. He pinched her arm. He pulled up the sleeve of her button-up. Track marks were clustered at her elbow crease like ant bites. She choked on the mac and cheese and woke up.

"You're banging it now?" Dessie said.

"What?"

"You're shooting up now," he said and pointed to her arm.

"Oh...yeah. Just a little." Her face was covered in cheese.

He thought about her body shrinking and cheeks getting sucked in. He thought about her clothes sagging off her. "Are you gonna die?" he said.

"Dessie, of course not," she said and put her hand on his back.

"You promise?"

She got out of the chair and crouched down and hugged him. "I promise." Cheese got on his neck and in his hair.

"Dad promised."

"Well, I'm not your dad," she said. "I loved him, but Dessie, he was full of shit."

"What do you mean?" He couldn't look in her eyes.

"Honey, Jefferson didn't build the Monticello house."

"Yes, he did!"

"It was slaves, Dessie," she said and rubbed his back. "Monticello was a plantation."

* * *

The next day, Dessie spent lunch in Felder's office, and during recess, he talked to Ms. Clemson about the plan.

When the kids came back in, Ms. Clemson said she had a special announcement. "First of all, I just want to say how proud I am of y'all for all the great work you've done this year. I think you deserve to give yourselves a big pat on the back."

All the kids smacked their backs. "Okay, that's enough," Ms. Clemson said. They were still wound up from recess and kept slapping themselves. "Enough," she snapped. "Now, it's come to the attention of Principal Felder and us teachers that we've been doing so well as a school that we've actually already covered all the material we need to learn for the whole year."

"What?" Cory said.

"So now we have an option," she continued. "We can either keep studying and get a jump start on next year's studies, mostly math, or we could have recess all day for the rest of the year."

The class erupted, and Dessie smiled. Kids ran around the room and stood on their chairs. They whipped pencils up into the ceiling.

"Hold on. Just a second," Ms. Clemson said. "Everyone in their seats, now!" They slowly worked their way back to their desks.

"We can only have all-day recess if everyone agrees. We need to have a vote. Now, everyone who wants to play outside for the rest of the year, raise your hand." Hands shot up, and she walked down a row, counting everyone. "Looks like everyone. Wait. Cory. Your hand is down. You're voting no?"

He nodded, looking down.

"Okay, y'all. That's it. Cory voted no, so we won't be having recess all day. We instead will be jumping into next year's math."

The room was silent. Then tongues were stuck out. Spitballs were shot. Someone poked Cory in the ribs with a pencil.

* * *

During recess, no one wanted to play with Cory anymore. He sat on the bench in front of the swings by himself. One day, Dessie sat next to him. "You've been bored in class," Dessie said.

"Huh?"

"You've been bored in class. I can tell. You're not challenged. I get it. I find myself working ahead in the book."

Cory looked straight ahead.

"I admire you, ya know?" Dessie said and smiled. "The way you stick to your guns even though everyone pressures you to give in."

Cory shook his head. "I know what you're doing."

Dessie laughed. "What am I doing?'

"Everything. This isn't how school is supposed to be. The teachers are messed up. On drugs."

"You think so?"

"Yeah. My uncle's messed up on drugs. My mom doesn't let me see him."

"See. You know what you believe, and you stick to it. My dad, he believed in a lot of things. He was principled. He told me that without principles, we have nothing. But, ya know, everything he said, it's all I have now."

Cory looked at him, confused.

"I'm telling you it's no good," Dessie continued. "None of it is real. I mean, he died a little while ago. I don't have a dad anymore. Or a mom. I'm an orphan. You know what I mean?"

Cory shook his head. He got up from the bench. "I'm sorry," he said and walked away. Dessie dug a Vicodin out of his pocket and chewed on it and tasted its bitterness.

* * *

Dessie gave out opium to the teachers for free, and they got the teachers' lounge sweet and dank. Felder came in with the assistant superintendent and introduced him as James Melton. The teachers struggled out of their chairs one by one and went back to their classrooms. Melton sniffed the

82

air, and Dessie giggled at the shape he was in—pit stains on his navy button-down even though it was 70-something out. His black bangs were stuck to his forehead, his face the color of mayo.

He sat opposite Felder and set his work bag on the table. Dessie stared at him. "I'm sorry. Is this your son here with us?" Melton asked Felder.

"No, this is Desmond. He's a student here, and he also likes to help out with administrative tasks."

"Oh."

"He's wildly precocious, and I can rely on him as much as anyone."

Dessie shook Melton's hand.

"Okay, well..." Melton said, then snorted with laughter. "Okay, now, what is that smell? It's wonderful. Potpourri?"

Felder nodded, and Melton slouched in his chair like he was at home. "Okay," he said again. "I have bad news, of course. We have to shut y'all down." Felder's face didn't change. "But you knew that, right? I mean, there are barely enough students here to justify keeping it open anyway, then you add in all the other issues."

Dessie took a Bic out of his pocket and lit the candle on the table. Melton giggled again, and his face regained some color. Dessie brought the pipe up from his lap and set the bowl in the flame to cook. Melton watched him take in the smoke and hold it in his lungs.

"What?" was all Melton could say, and Dessie exhaled in his face.

"Opium," Dessie said.

"Hmm," Melton said and slouched further into his chair, and his eyelids drooped. Dessie blew another cloud in his face. Dad would say that morphine is literally pleasure. It unlocks the pleasure potential that already exists in our brains, and that to be against it was to be against joy itself.

Dessie fought off the nods and set the pipe and candle in front of Melton on the table. Felder laughed and took out her camera phone. "Wait," Dessie said and went to Melton and messed up his hair a little. He gently pulled down on the man's lower lip, and saliva dripped down his chin.

"Dessie, you're a goddamn genius," Felder said and took pictures from different angles. Dessie took his stash out of his backpack and weighed out a quarter-ounce on the triple-beam scale taken from the science supply closet. He swept it neatly into a sandwich baggie and tied it off and set it in Melton's shirt pocket.

* * *

There were only eight students left in Ms. Clemson's class. They were the only class still doing schoolwork, and they would hear the other kids outside playing. Anger toward Cory grew stronger every day. Instead of spitballs, the kids threw coins, and at lunch, he would eat as much as he could in line before someone could knock his tray over.

Dessie split his time between 107 and outside. He was glad to have the teachers off synthetics, and with no teaching to do, they blew their paychecks on opium in no time. Mr. Lisicky was living in his classroom and hadn't changed clothes in a week. The patch in Dessie's backyard wasn't enough anymore. The field behind the swings was made off-limits to the kids, and Dessie showed the teachers how to plant and harvest poppies. He let them work in exchange for opium. Lisicky complained about his back, but Dessie reminded him that the best thing for pain was opium and whining wasn't going to get him any more of that.

One morning, Dessie went outside to find that the bright red poppy flowers had fallen to the ground. He gave the teachers the day off. He and Ms. Clemson went to the science supply closet and got jars and X-Acto knives. He showed her how to slit the bulbs all the way around. He didn't trust the other teachers to do it right. They spent all morning doing this, watching the white goo ooze out.

After lunch, they went back out, and the white goo had turned black. They carefully scraped it off into the jars and got sunburned in the spring sun. When they were done, the school day was nearly finished, and they went to the cafeteria, to the back, and drank Capri Suns from the big fridge.

"We gotta get rid of the pods tomorrow," Dessie said. "We oughta burn them."

They went home, and after dinner, Dessie turned the stove on low. He was about to put the resin in the pan to separate the opium from plant junk when the doorbell rang. He and Ms. Clemson looked at each other.

"Who could that be?" she said.

"No idea."

"Should we not answer?"

"No. We have to. The lights are on. Um," he said. "You answer. Say you're my babysitter if they ask and Dad is out of town on business."

She answered the door with Dessie behind her. It was a woman in her thirties in a gray skirt suit. She was cheery and asked if Dad was in, and Ms. Clemson told her he was on a business trip.

"And is this Desmond here?" the woman said and leaned down.

He acted shy and half-hid behind Ms. Clemson. "Hi," he said and took her hand.

"Do y'all happen to have his cell phone number off-hand?"

"Um, sure," Ms. Clemson said and took out her phone and read off the number. The woman said thank you and got in her car and left.

Ms. Clemson ran her fingers through her hair over and over. Dessie went back to the opium and made sure not to burn it. He thought about his conversation with Cory, what Dad said about loose lips. He thought about Cory talking to his mom.

He put Dad's phone on its charger, and soon it buzzed.

* * *

The teachers chopped off the heads of all the poppy plants with garden shears they brought from home. They made a big pile. They'd wait until night to burn it so no one would see the smoke. Dessie mostly stayed in class that morning. Ms. Clemson told him Felder needed to talk to him, but he didn't feel like talking. The classroom phone kept ringing.

"Tell her I'll come in later," he said.

During recess, he sat on a swing, and Ms. Clemson came outside and found him.

"You gotta go see her. She's getting pissed."

He shrugged.

"Listen. She said there's gonna be another inspection.

86

Melton got fired. He's strung out. The actual superintendent is coming. Other parents are complaining."

"The kids can't keep their mouths shut," he said and kicked mulch. "I've been dreaming a lot lately."

"What?" she said and sighed. She sat on the swing next to his.

"I've been having a lot of dreams at night."

"Yeah? What about?"

"Nothing. Boring stuff. Like I'll just be at home, mostly. I'll be sitting on the couch, watching TV, or eating dinner. But it'll feel so real, ya know?"

"I have dreams like that, yeah."

"And I'll just know things, like how you just know things? Like you know your car is out in the parking lot right now even though you can't see it."

She nodded.

"In my dreams, everything is like it normally is except Dad is alive. He's not with me, and I can't see him, but I know he's in his room or out doing something. I'm not even thinking about him, but I know he's alive. Then I wake up."

The chains of his swing squeaked as he bobbed in place. "Dessie, you gotta go see the principal," she said.

"Okay, just another five minutes," he said and leaned forward and pushed off the mulch. He kicked his legs out and then tucked them under. With each swing, Dessie got a little higher. He was gonna see how high he could get.

Always Be My Baby

Freddy, the big eight-year-old, paced the yard, seething in the noon heat. "Tell me something, Freddy," Hannah said. "What's going on for you right now?" He closed his eyes and punched the air. He was searching, trying. Hannah had been working with him on expressing himself. He screamed and charged at the lumpy vases with his fists balled up.

"No, Freddy!" she said and stood in his way. "Use this." She handed him the bat and turned her back as he brought it down on the vase. He crushed the other one too and kicked over the fold-out table they'd sat on. He threw off his goggles and raised the bat over his head with both hands and tried to break it over his knee. The wood stayed solid though, and he went to the ground, crying and grabbing at his leg.

She hurried to his side and looked over at Lynn

and clenched her teeth. He was still sitting in his lawn chair, smoking a cigarette with his legs crossed. She told him to go to the kitchen and fix a bag of ice. She ended the session a little early and said bye to the other clients.

She brought Freddy inside and sat him on the couch and gave him an ice cream sandwich. She'd been working with him for nine months, since he beat up another boy during recess and stuffed mulch in his mouth.

He sighed when the doorbell rang. Hannah answered the door, and he walked past her and past his mom, Gloria, and waited by the green minivan. Gloria had told her once that she got it because she thought she'd have a bunch of kids.

"He just got back from his father's," Gloria said. Hannah figured, but she didn't want to talk about it then. They'd go over it in painful detail on Monday during their one-on-one session. "If I could kill him and get away with it, I swear."

Hannah nodded along until she said bye.

"Those vases were shitty," Lynn said as soon as she shut the door.

"What? What were you doing?"

"What?"

"You just sat there while he was hurt."

"I wanted to do something," he said, looking down. "I just froze up like I do." It was the lithium that caused his lapses, Hannah knew. It was his baby so she let him watch. He called it Smash Therapy. It was a dumb idea, but it was important to him. She didn't have the heart to tell him that rage rooms were already a thing. He thought he'd thought of it.

"I know what you're thinking," he said. "But my vision for Smash Therapy remains true."

The vision shit again. He got fixated on things. The other day she found a DVD of *The Secret* in the dresser and threw it away.

"I wish you could see what I see," he said. "Freddy tried to break the bat because the vases were garbage. They weren't satisfying to smash, so he tried to break this fine wooden sculpture," he said and stroked the bat.

She took it out of his hands and swang it, just joking, but he didn't move away, and it hit his thigh just right.

He cried out and hopped on his other leg and fell on the floor. He laughed. "You fucking…"

She laughed too. "Fucking what?"

"You gave me a dead leg. It's going numb." He squirmed on the floor like he'd been shot then froze and closed his eyes. Hannah got down next to him and undid his belt. She slid his pants down and put him in her mouth. He came back to life with a gasp. He was being cute, and they went to bed. No matter what she did though, she couldn't get him more than a little stiff. It was the lithium.

* * *

The next morning, Hannah woke up to Whitney Houston. "The Greatest Love of All" was blaring from the garage. It was part of this playlist Lynn would have on repeat. There were only two other songs on it: "Hero" by Mariah Carey and "Beautiful" by Christina Aguilera. He was on this self-love kick, saying you can never really have anyone but yourself so you better make sure you at least have you.

Hannah got up and went to the garage. When she opened the door, she could smell the mania—wet clay, cigarette smoke, sweat. Lynn sat shirtless on the little stool at the pottery wheel. The floor was covered in newspaper, and his forearms were specked with clay and paint. She had to park her Civic in the driveway to make room. His old Eclipse was on the street in front of the house. He took a big swig from his coffee thermos and didn't notice her there.

She hit the button for the garage door, and it startled him. She turned the volume down on the boombox. "It needs to air out in here," she said. He ran up to her like a dog and kissed her and cupped her ass in his big hands. He'd been up all night and had BO, but they hadn't had sex in months. She knew he hadn't taken his meds.

"The hero that Mariah is talking about is actually just herself," he said. "I never knew that until recently. Did you know?"

"Yes."

"We all have a hero inside us. I believe that."

One of the unpainted pieces looked stepped on. "Yeah, that one collapsed in the oven," he said before she could ask. He cooked all the pieces in the kitchen oven. It took forever and had to be at the highest possible temperature. The gas bills were ridiculous. They never used it for food anyway.

"We can't afford to waste clay," Hannah said. "This stuff isn't cheap." It was cheap, like the stuff you had in art class, but they were broke, floating a couple credit cards.

The thing on the wheel shouldn't have been able to stand. The bottom was like a little salsa bowl, upside-down, and on top of that was a thin beam holding up a big salad-kinda-bowl.

She pointed at it. "That's wonderful, sugar."

"Not sure how I'm gonna get it in the oven," he said. She didn't know why he didn't just make the big bowl first and have it as the bottom then turn it over after it cooked. She didn't have the heart to bring this up.

"Let it dry a little first, maybe," she said, but he wasn't listening. He was looking for something. He bent over and picked up a little black vase with pink hearts on it.

"Hearts because I love you," he said and gave it to her.

"Aww," she said and kissed him and grabbed his cock.

"I don't need you," he said. "Every day I choose to be with you."

She had an appointment with Gloria at ten, but she took him into the shower with her anyway. They both came quick like it'd been waiting just under the surface. Lynn groaned and let the wall tile hold him up.

They were ready again after they toweled off. She couldn't explain to Gloria over the phone right then. She texted her that Lynn had burned his hand bad on the oven, and they'd have to reschedule. It said *Sent 9:23 a.m.* It was a hard flake, and she knew Gloria was probably coming apart. She barely made it from one session to the next. She didn't have anyone else.

* * *

Lynn got up and left the bedroom around noon, and Hannah heard his playlist back on in the garage. She hollered at him, "Let it dry awhile."

She got up and checked her phone. Gloria had texted

back. *Jesus. I was about to leave the house.* They rescheduled for the next morning. Hannah got her blowdryer from the bathroom and went to the garage. She found the extension cord, and she got the surface of the big vase somewhat hard. They picked up the whole wheel and set it on the open oven door. On three, they lifted the piece and got it on the rack. He gave her a double high-five and wanted sex again, but she was too sore.

He wasn't on anything the first couple years they dated, and she would ride the waves. She'd never tell him this, but she liked it better when he was depressed. He'd stay in bed and she'd hold him and they'd listen to Townes Van Zandt— the saddest, prettiest songs.

After he got diagnosed, he said he didn't want to have kids and pass it on. She fought him, but he stuck to it. He said he didn't care what she said; he'd done the research and there was definitely a hereditary component. The more time she spent with Freddy, the more she didn't mind. A kid could end up any kind of way, and you'd be stuck with them.

Lynn said he was starving all of a sudden, and she followed him to the kitchen. He dug through the fridge and ate lunch meat and cheese slices with no bread. "You're like a dog," she said. "Sit down, and I'll make you a sandwich."

From the dining room table, he yelled out all the food he wanted. "Please, honey," he said. He wanted chips and salsa with the sandwich, Oreos, and ice cream if they had any left. He didn't ask for Dr. Pepper, but she poured him a tall glass and stirred in some cherry Benadryl. He could have a long nap. He'd been working so hard.

* * *

Gloria said Freddy called her a bitch the other day for not letting him stay up late to play video games. She sat in the vinyl chair with her palms pasted to the armrests. She was a small woman, and her feet just touched the ground. Hannah imagined Fred Sr. referring to her as "that bitch" to Freddy over and over. Gloria said she didn't play that game anymore, wouldn't call him a bastard in front of their son.

"I wanna shoot a gun," she said and fidgeted.

Hannah was startled but didn't show it. It made sense. People are attracted to guns when they feel impotent or powerless in their lives. Hannah explained this to her. I'm a great psychologist, she thought.

"Yeah," Gloria said. "I feel stuck." Her voice cracked as she started to cry. "I just feel like I've lost Freddy, and I'll never get him back." She wiped her eyes with her sleeve.

"I think that's natural," Hannah said. There were eight minutes left in the session, but it seemed like a good stopping point. "I think we should continue this conversation tomorrow."

Gloria shook her head. "What's the point?" she said. "All this talking."

Hannah stood up and went over and hugged her. She was coming two to three times a week at $110 per session.

Walking out to the minivan, Hannah explained to her the importance of surrendering to the healing process. It never happens as fast as we want. Right then, Lynn pulled up in the Eclipse. He hopped out and waved at Gloria. He popped the trunk and grabbed bags of groceries with both hands. Hannah should've wrapped one in medical tape.

"He tries to be so tough," Hannah said. Gloria shook her head and got in the van and took off.

Hannah grabbed the mail on the way back in. There was a letter from the homeowners' association, a noise violation warning from the date of the last Smash Therapy session. It said another violation would be a $500 fine.

Lynn asked her what it was, and she told him nothing and tossed it in the recycling bin. It was her idea to come out to the Northside suburbs with these people. She'd told him not to worry about a mortgage.

She helped put the food away and saw the box of red wine. She held it up and looked at him.

"It's been so long since we cut loose," he said. "We've been working so hard. I think it would actually be good for us." It really had been a long time. They deserved it.

"Don't worry," he said. "I'll get my sculpting done first."

He was so cute. He thought he was some professional sculptor. She didn't know if she'd be able to tell him he might have to get a job soon, any job.

"I don't think a little wine while you work would hurt," she said. She took out two glasses and rinsed the dust out in the sink. She poured them half-full, and they said cheers and clinked the glasses together.

"That's so good. Goddamn," he said. They headed to the garage, and she sat on the old desk while he got started on the wheel. She asked him if he wanted his playlist on.

"Seriously?"

"It's totally fine," she said.

She turned it on and sang along. She loved Mariah Carey when she was a kid. She remembered she was in

96

fourth grade when *Daydream* came out. It was the one with "Fantasy" and "Always Be My Baby." Everyone had it, and the songs played on the radio nonstop.

Sitting there, she was taken aback by what all Lynn had made in the last couple days. There was a gold trophy with a football on it. He'd made a clay HDTV painted black. They were things you wanted to smash. She wanted to spike the football trophy right there on the concrete floor.

Christina Aguilera came on again, and she remembered the binder with all her old CDs. It was somewhere in the garage in a box. She went to the kitchen to refill their glasses and came back and started going through the junk.

She found the case in the box with all of Lynn's baseball cards. She flipped through the pages and recognized the CD's plain olive front right away. Lynn went "Hey!" when she stopped his playlist, but she told him to hush. The first song was "Fantasy."

The very beginning was just Mariah cooing into the mic. "What's this?" he said, but then the beat hit. "Oh shit!"

Hannah finished off her glass and started dancing. He got up, and they grinded on each other. They took the stereo to the kitchen and danced on the linoleum.

* * *

She got woken up in the morning by Lynn yelling from the bed. Someone was knocking at the door, and he was telling them to go away. He got out of bed. Hannah opened her eyes, and she remembered Gloria. The clock said 10:08 a.m. Their session was for ten.

"Stop, honey. Don't move," she said and got up. He stopped right before the kitchen where Gloria would've been able to see him from the front door window. He looked mad, and Hannah dragged him back to bed. "It's Gloria," she said. Her head throbbed. Even in college, she got the worst hangovers.

"What're you gonna do?" he asked.

"Nothing," she said and took one of his Camels from the pack. It was awful, and she gave it to him after two puffs. She wouldn't be able to fall back asleep. She needed weed. Gloria knocked one more time. Hannah waited a few minutes then went out to the kitchen, and the van was gone.

She went to the living room and looked out to the street and realized Gloria would've seen both of their cars outside. "What the fuck am I gonna tell her?"

"You could tell her the truth," he said, looking down. "You had too much wine."

No. That was no good. "I could say I lost track of time, and we went on a run." That would explain the cars.

He shook his head. She could say she took some new kind of cold medicine that just knocked her out and made her sleep through her alarm.

"Yeah, that could maybe work," he said. He pointed at the kitchen table and told her to sit down; he was making breakfast. He brought her a cup of coffee, and she massaged her temples.

She needed to put something in her stomach, but the smell of the bacon cooking made her nauseous. Lynn wasn't paying attention to it. He was squinting at the front window. She turned her head to see. The minivan was back. "Oh shit," she said. She pointed to the bedroom and told Lynn to go.

She turned off the stove and heard footsteps on the walkway. She ducked down behind the cabinets. She reached up and grabbed the pan with the smoking bacon.

Lynn peeked around the corner.

"Stay back!" she whispered.

He looked at her like she was crazy.

"She's been acting weird," she said. "Last session she said she wants to get a gun. Her face was cold when she said it."

"Did you tell her it would be better to do Smash Therapy instead?"

She didn't respond. She was afraid to look over the counter to see if the car was still there. They sat in silence for about five minutes.

Lynn lay on the floor, flat on his belly. "Don't worry," he said, grinning for some reason. He started crawling on his belly.

"No, don't," she said, but he was already moving past her. He looked ridiculous, and she covered her mouth to muffle her laugh. He got to the door and sat up against it.

"I think she's gone," he mouthed to her.

She went to stand up, but suddenly his eyes got big. He put his finger to his lips and waved at her to go back. She heard the footsteps. The screen door creaked and slapped back shut. The footsteps moved away.

He stood slowly. "The van's gone," he said. Hannah hurried over and surveyed the street through the window. She opened the door, and there was a folded piece of paper at her feet.

It was a letter from Gloria. "What's it say?" Lynn said.

"*I'm looking for a new therapist,*" Hannah read out loud.

"No way!" he said. "Why?"

"I told you we shouldn't have drank that wine," she said and went to grab her phone. "What should I tell her?" She sat on the couch and dialed without a plan. She told Gloria she was sick last night and took some Benadryl and overslept.

"I don't know. I don't think I believe you," Gloria said. She'd never talked like that to Hannah before. Hannah told her this was just her attachment issues flaring up again. It had nothing to do with Hannah and everything to do with Gloria's dad going on long business trips when she was a kid.

Gloria said, "You're the one who told me to cut toxic people out of my life."

Hannah put her hand over the receiver. "Goddamnit." She took a breath. "It's your decision," she said and got up from the couch. "But I have to be honest, Gloria. I'm taken aback by how selfish you're being right now. Me and Freddy are just beginning to form trust, and you're gonna sever that. He's already got attachment issues."

Gloria sighed. She said she'd think about it and hung up.

"What a bitch," Hannah said. "Why'd you have to get that goddamn wine?"

"We manifested this reality," he said. "You're sabotaging your relationship with Gloria for some reason. It's for the best even if you can't see the purpose right now."

He had the most self-satisfied smile. He went to the garage with his cup of coffee, and she followed him.

"Are you watching *The Secret* again?" she said.

He sat at his stool. "You stole my DVD, didn't you?"

"Forget about these vases," she said. "We're not doing another session. I got a warning from the HOA."

He stared at her. "Forget about the vases?" He looked like he wanted to say something else but held it in. He got up and took his keys from the kitchen counter and went out the front door.

She sat on the couch and took out her phone and checked her email. She looked through her cell phone contacts, looking for old clients. She called two of them but neither picked up. She left voicemails asking them how they were doing and said it would be great to catch up.

* * *

Lynn hadn't come back by the next morning, and she was pretty sure he was at HEB. He went there to think sometimes. The parking lot was so big they never noticed if you'd been there forever.

She called Gloria, and she was a little more reasonable this time. She agreed to drop Freddy off so Hannah could at least have a closing session with him.

He was even more unresponsive than usual. He just stared down at the rug in her office. His hair looked recently buzzed, and she asked him about it but nothing. Gloria must've said something to him.

"This is pretty boring, Freddy. I'm bored. How about you?"

He nodded.

"Why do you think it's boring?"

He shrugged his shoulders. "It's always boring," he

said. She explained that it was only as boring as he made it. It was only boring because he wasn't engaged.

"What?" he said. She felt like working with low-caliber kids was pointless sometimes. They could really struggle with easy concepts.

She sat up on the edge of her seat and leaned toward him. She said, "Wanna go smash some shit?"

He smiled and nodded.

She had him wait in the office while she set everything up in the backyard. She grabbed the football trophy and set it on the table. She almost dropped the clay TV, lugging it out there, and she put out the other random vases too.

She hollered for Freddy to come on back to the yard. He ran out and stopped in front of her. She held the bat above his head. He jumped for it a few times before she let him have it. She stood in the way. He paced in the yard and tried to get past her. She kept telling him he wasn't allowed to touch the pottery.

He hit the ground with the bat and grunted. His face burned red. She finally stepped aside, and he yelled and charged straight at the TV. He cracked it with the first shot, and it fell to the ground. He bashed it over and over until it was just shards. He smashed the football trophy. He was out of breath and leaned against the fence.

She took the bat from him and walked up to the big salad-bowl vase. She closed her eyes and swang. It jarred her hands but felt good.

"Give it back," he said. She handed it over, and he finished off what was left. The yard was covered in pieces of clay. She gave him a double high-five and brushed the dust off his shirt.

They went inside, and she wiped his arms and face with a wet paper towel. They heard a honk from out front.

"So you're gonna tell your mom what a great time you had, right?"

He smiled and shrugged and walked out the door. She went out to the porch and waved to Gloria, but she drove off without waving back. Hannah stood there for a minute, thinking maybe she'd turn around and come back.

Lynn still hadn't come back when she started getting hungry for dinner, and she wondered if something had happened to him, if maybe he wasn't at HEB. She decided to drive by to see if his car was in the parking lot.

She drove the two miles, and there the Eclipse was in the back row. She had the idea to scare him so she parked on the other side near the front.

She crept up to the car and slapped the window. He jumped, and she pointed at him and laughed. He rolled down the window.

"You startled me, but you didn't surprise me," he said. "I envisioned you coming for me." The ground by the window was littered with Camel stubs, and the floorboard was covered in empty chicken salad containers and Snickers wrappers. "I'm depressed," he said.

She opened the door. The car was gross, and he hadn't showered, but she climbed on top of him anyway.

Her knees hit against the door and the console, but she kept going until he finished. She rolled over to the passenger seat and caught her breath.

"Rage rooms," he said. He was staring straight ahead.

"What?"

"Did you know about them? Be honest."

"Yeah. How'd you find out?"

He shook his head. "I was talking with the greeter. It doesn't matter. Were you ever gonna tell me?"

"Sorry. What we do is different though. We talk through emotions while we smash stuff. It's a lot better."

"I dunno."

She told him to go home and shower and she'd go inside and get stuff for dinner. She went to the heat lamps and took one of the rotisserie chickens and got a tub of mustard potato salad and a can of green beans.

When she got to the house, she found him in the backyard holding clay shards.

"It was for therapy. I'm sorry," she said. "Freddy came over."

He went to the garage. "Man, he really smashed everything?"

"He had a lot of rage built up," she said. "But I think it really helped."

She set the table and tore the wings off the chicken and put them both on his plate. She heated their plates up in the microwave and called for him.

They ate and Lynn moved the potatoes around the plate with his fork. He was mad at her. "There were a few I made for myself, the TV," he said.

"I was trying to make it where Freddy would tell Gloria he wanted to come back."

"I've always wondered how it'd feel to smash the screen of a big TV with a baseball bat," he said.

She picked up her plate and threw it across the room like a frisbee. It dented the plaster wall and shattered on the ground. Lynn's eyes got crazy, and he smashed his plate too. She went into the kitchen and picked up the blender. He threw the coffee mugs against the wall. They moved on to the living room, and she went to get the bat.

Inside Recess

Eric had a retainer and glasses with the strap-thing that went around his neck, but he'd eat anything you told him to—crayons, pencils, homework packets with the staples, his boogers, your boogers, anything. That's why we let him sit with us. We stayed in the cafeteria until the teachers shooed us outside. It was November and crazy cold out, but I think they figured it was okay because it wasn't snowing yet. They needed their break from us.

Eric was one of the ones who hid in the bathroom stalls. He sat on a toilet and read his fantasy books. Most of us played soccer even though we didn't really like it or know how to play. Hundreds of us chased one ball with our hands in our pockets just to keep warm.

By December, the snow came up to our waists, and the teachers finally gave us inside recess. Everything we'd gotten into since kindergarten got popular again. Ainsley brought back Cat's Cradle. She was the only one who could do the actual Cat's Cradle trick, and we made a circle around her while she gave her seminars. My best friend, Ben, was the best with the yoyo—around the world, rock the baby and all that. I was a Pogs fiend. I had the inch-thick rubber Super Slammer, and I'd smash through piles of them. We played for keeps, and soon I had every Pog in our class. They could buy them back with cash or snacks.

We hadn't gone outside for recess in over a week, and I could tell we were getting to Mr. Perry. He stared at the solitaire game on his computer screen and scratched his bald head until there were red spots. He was the coolest teacher and never got mad, but he started ignoring us. Ainsley was the only one he'd talk to, so all questions and bathroom requests had to go through her. She handled everything so well—running the class, her seminars, and somehow finding time to train for the Presidential Fitness Challenge coming up in the spring. She did diamond push-ups in the corner and slipped out of class to run up and down the stairs. She wore overalls every day, and her one pigtail would magically switch sides when you looked away.

The next week, Eric's dad surprised him during lunch with a huge cardboard box he was out of breath from carrying. He looked just like he should've, goofy glasses and blue slacks. We fought to read the label on the side of the box—*K'NEX* in big letters. I'd only ever seen K'NEX in commercials. They were like Legos for older, smarter kids. You had to be really smart to do them. Eric dug through the bags of pieces and found the instructions. It was the new roller coaster set with three loops, a massive undertaking.

Eric tried to set up the site in our classroom on the tile

floor by the sink, but Ben and the other guys kept stealing bags of pieces and playing keep away. "C'mon, guys!" Eric said, reaching with his little arms.

"He's playing right into their hands," Ainsley whispered to me, and we came up with a plan. She went and talked softly with Mr. Perry for a minute and came back to announce that the tiled area was reserved for Eric and his roller coaster. We had to have his permission to touch anything, "and, um, if we can't handle that we'll have silent recess until Christmas break," she added. She was smart and brave and pretty. The truth was that Mr. Perry didn't care what we did anymore. We could come and go from the classroom whenever, but everyone sat on the edge of the carpet and watched Eric separate the pieces into different piles.

I went to check out a high-stakes Pogs game I heard fifth grader Philip Haskins was running out of Mrs. Moore's room. She was asleep in her chair, and the desks were pushed to the walls to make room for everyone crowding the game. A few looked up at me like I must've been lost, but I opened my backpack and showed them the foot-long tubes of Pogs, and they cleared a path for me.

They threw official Pogs around like they were Tootsie Rolls. Philip declared my Super Slammer illegal, so I had to use a thin plastic one like everyone else. I was nothing without it, and I lost everything—first my official Pogs, then all my off-brand ones.

I retreated back to the classroom, and Ainsley was too busy helping Eric to notice how sad I was, even when I stood over her holding the empty tubes. They worked fast without talking, and soon the foundation began to take shape. I dropped my Super Slammer on the carpet and said I didn't want it anymore, and the guys fought for it. I sat in the corner by the window where me and Ainsley held each other after Sonny the class gerbil died, where we'd almost kissed once. I watched the snow pile up and wished it was summer. I wanted to go as high as I could on the swings and forget the room.

I couldn't keep away from the action though, and the next day I got sucked into a Pog game with some first graders. They didn't understand all the rules, and it was hard to keep them focused. I'd just lost the PB&J sandwich Mom packed for my lunch when Ainsley found me.

"I'm sorry," I told her. "I'll never touch another Pog again."

"Eric wants you on the crew," she said.

"Seriously?" I was so grateful. I hoped it was her idea.

Eric put me in charge of the pieces. I had to sort them by shape and hand them to him and Ainsley when they asked. Ainsley was totally locked in. She said the piece she needed and reached back without even looking at me. I understood. We all were jealous of her spot.

We didn't have class time at all anymore. Mr. Perry stopped playing solitaire. He sat with the kids and watched us. "We didn't have K'NEX growing up," he said. Christmas break was coming up fast, and Eric constantly reminded us about the deadline we had to hit. *12/15* took up the whole dry erase board. I got Ben on the crew, and he took over the pieces. I finally got to help build it. Eric sat on the counter by the sink and directed us. We trusted his vision. The lunch bell didn't ring, and we worked straight into the afternoon. Our fingertips callused from snapping the hard plastic

110

together.

We made huge progress every day, and the structure got bigger and bigger but didn't look any more like a roller coaster than before. I didn't want it to seem like I was questioning his judgment, but I had to ask Eric if I could take a quick look at the instructions. "Oh, I threw those away forever ago," he said.

Mr. Perry agreed with Eric that only people working on the project should be allowed inside the classroom. Mr. Perry wanted to work on it too, but Eric said his fingers were too big to handle the pieces, so he had to sit in the hallway like everyone else. Everyone waited outside the doorway and begged for a chance, including Philip Haskins and his crew of fifth graders who'd bullied their way to the front.

After working all morning one day, Eric let me and Ainsley go for a bathroom break. We took turns drinking from the water fountain.

"I dunno about Eric," I said. "I think he's losing it."

She checked down the halls. "You better be careful, talking like that."

"I'm just saying...it doesn't look like the picture on the box, and we have way more pieces, I think. Where did they come from?"

"You need to keep your head down. Any kid would kill to take your spot." She tugged on my shirt. "We gotta get back."

When we came back Mr. Perry was blocking the doorway. He stepped aside for Ainsley but put his hand out to me.

"Project workers only," he said.

"I'm with Eric. Just ask him," I said and tried to get

past, but he grabbed my shoulder. "Eric was the one who instructed me not to let you through."

I looked at Ainsley. "That's impossible," I said. "I've been nothing but loyal and hardworking."

He just nodded toward the mass of kids behind me.

"Ainsley," I pleaded. "Talk to him." But her eyes promised nothing.

I walked down the rows of kids lining the hallway and got pelted with spitballs. A protractor whizzed past my head and shattered on the wall.

I sat down at the end of the line and looked at my watch—*December 25*. We missed the deadline. Ben was sitting across the hall from me, head hanging, lips moving.

"Ben," I said. He didn't respond. "Ben!"

"Huh?"

"Ben, it's me."

He nodded.

"What did you want for Christmas?" I said.

"Christmas?" he said, confused. "I dunno. K'NEX."

* * *

I didn't know how much time had passed when I woke up. Someone had made off with my watch. Kids were strewn all down the hallway, some asleep, others talking to themselves. Mr. Perry was rocking back and forth in front of the classroom. He had lost a lot of weight, and he pulled on his side hair until it stuck straight out.

There was shouting coming from inside the classroom. It was probably what had woken me up. I stood up and walked to the door. It sounded like Ainsley, but I'd never heard her yell like that before. The door shot open, and she appeared. She slammed the door behind her and stomped away. I heard Eric smashing things in the room. Soon it was quiet again. I put my ear to the door but couldn't hear anything.

I jumped when someone touched my back. It was Ainsley, shaking her head. "You were right," she said. "He's crazy."

I didn't know what to say.

"He fired me," she said. "After all I did for the project."

I turned away from her.

"I'm sorry," she said, but I kept my back to her until she left, stumbling down the hallway. She sat against the wall, at the end of the line, and hugged her legs.

I looked at Mr. Perry again, his sucked-in cheeks, and remembered how hungry I was. Once I thought of it, I couldn't get it out of my mind.

I wandered the school and tried every doorknob and went into every unlocked classroom. I knocked desks over and emptied them out onto the floor. I rifled through teachers' drawers and feasted on bags of leftover Halloween candy. This only awoke my hunger, and I was drawn to the cafeteria.

Then I thought about Ainsley, how her overalls hung on her shoulders like on a hanger. I turned around and went back to the classroom. She was like I'd left her, and I nudged with my foot. "C'mon," I said and helped her up, and she didn't say anything.

We went to the cafeteria and climbed over the counter and found a case of chocolate milk in the fridge and fish patties in the freezer. We stared at the frying patties in the pan and took them off while they were still cold inside.

We sat at the table we always sat at and stuffed the patties in our mouths with our hands and chugged chocolate milk and chucked the little empty cartons on the floor. There was enough to last us forever. She smiled at me, and we looked into each other's eyes. We had a staring contest, and she made a pig face, and I laughed. We played again, but my mind wandered. I couldn't help but wonder if Eric had finished, if the cart could really go around the loops and not fall off the tracks. How big was it?

I thought I heard something like a faraway gasp, but I didn't trust my senses anymore. Ainsley's eyes got shifty, and she pushed her tray away. She massaged her stomach and burped. There was another gasp, maybe.

"You hear that?" she said.

"Something, yeah. I don't care."

She stood up and stepped over the table bench. "I just feel like standing," she said.

Then she took off. I chased after her, but she was in such better shape. All that chocolate milk sloshing around in my stomach gave me a cramp, and I had to stop and walk. The gasps echoed louder through the dark halls, louder and louder, Mr. Perry's deep gasp. I turned the corner onto our hallway and was blinded by the light coming from the open doorway. Ainsley made some kind of sound, but I couldn't tell what it meant.

She didn't turn her head away from it when I came in. My eyes cleared up, and the K'NEX structure was bigger than Mr. Perry. It was the head of a smiling girl. It was beautiful and had one pigtail, an ode to Eric's secret love.

Eric walked up to Ainsley and fidgeted and pushed

114

up his glasses. She took his hand and led him inside it. She closed the little door, and they made noise like none of us were there.

You're Gonna Know My Name

There'd been many graphic photos, but Lucy was the only one who'd shown up to the press conference in the park. Mayor Gottlieb flipped through his notecards and set them back down on the beat-up wooden podium. It looked straight out of a school cafeteria.

Lucy felt bad for him. "It's just because of the Henry Phillips thing," she said. The JonBenét Ramsey stuff was just dying down when Henry Phillips got kidnapped. He was the four-year-old son of Victor Phillips, a big casino CEO in Vegas. The kidnappers demanded three million in the ransom note.

Gottlieb asked her where she was from.

"*Lucy on Laughlin*, sir."

"What?"

"It's a TV show. I'm Lucy."

He looked at his notecards again then back at her.

"That's public access or what?"

"Channel 18, the community channel."

He smirked and shook his head and pushed his glasses up with his finger. Then he, the mayor of Laughlin, Nevada, stepped away from the old podium and headed to his car.

"You're just gonna big-time me like that?" Lucy yelled. He waved a dismissive hand at her.

He must've remembered the podium was his because he turned back and looked at her like she'd planned on stealing it. She filmed him as he carried it on his back across the patches of yellow grass and loaded it into the back of his Lincoln Town Car. He was supposed to address the recent front-page spread in *The Laughlin Gazette* about a cockfighting show that was openly held at the abandoned GoldSky Casino.

"What an asshole," Lucy said and packed her camera back into the rolly cart. Gottlieb looked like a real mayor though, she thought, with his full head of white hair. Her arthritis was acting up again, and she took her time dragging the cart to the F-250. Her brother Curtis let her use the truck on the weekends and sometimes at night. He didn't like to leave the house when he wasn't at his demo job. He wouldn't admit he had depression.

He was half-asleep on the couch when she got home, and copies of the *Globe* and the *Enquirer* were on the coffee table. Both covers had the same school picture of little Henry Phillips smiling with his front teeth missing. Curtis didn't stir when Lucy sat on the other side of the couch. *Cops* was on the TV. It was their favorite show, and he liked to imitate the way the drunk people talked. This episode was in Philadelphia, and this drunk driver wouldn't pull over.

He wasn't speeding; he was just swerving and not paying attention to the cop blaring his siren. Lucy couldn't enjoy it. She was still fuming about Gottlieb. He thought he was too good for her show—like he had anything else to do.

She wondered why Laughlin even had a mayor. She would leave the bullshit town soon. She'd move to Vegas or anywhere where there were more people, more action—a place where they filmed *Cops*. Her mind raced, and she got an idea and got excited. She clapped her hands together loud, and Curtis' eyes opened. "He's alive," she said. He grunted and sat up. He asked where the episode was at.

"Did you know Laughlin has a mayor?" she asked.

"Yeah, because of you."

"But would you otherwise?"

"No way. It doesn't make sense."

"I bet nobody knows, right?" She wanted to do a survey for the show that showed nobody knew who Gottlieb was because fuck him. She needed to be so excited that Curtis would think it wasn't worth fighting her. She didn't want to go back out alone, plus she needed him to keep a lookout for casino security.

It was hard because he worked and she didn't. Like the Disability Office, he didn't believe someone in their thirties could have arthritis. He said it was just because she was out of shape. She was still fighting the case, and when she finally got her money, it was off to Vegas. She hadn't told anyone this, but one day she would be a cameraman for *Cops*. She was building up her tape roll to send to Fox. She just had to get partial disability and Medicare to get the right meds so she could get into shape. For training, she could run up hills with her camera on her shoulder.

When it went to commercial, she jumped in front of the TV and did her spiel.

"That's shitty," Curtis said. "He's already there. Might as well talk to you."

"Seriously."

He cocked his brow and got madder. "Who does he think he is, treating you like that? We are this town. He serves us. That's his duty."

She just had to get him off the couch. "We'll poll people on the strip. You can gamble some if you want."

He stood up, and she loaded the cart back into the truck cab. They drove the couple miles to the strip downtown and parked at Harrah's, the last major casino left. "Harrah's is no good," Lucy said. "It's mostly out-of-towners. We need locals."

He cut the engine and opened his door. "Oh well. We could use a little exercise in the sun," he said and got out. He waited with his arms crossed while she worked her way out of her seat and unloaded the cart.

They walked down the boardwalk along the river. The water was too blue for Nevada, reflecting off the crusty gold-and-silver buildings. Curtis went into Paradise first and waved her in. No one was watching. It was like she remembered, with its cigarette-burned green carpet and half-lit chandeliers. No one manned the roulette wheel, Curtis' favorite, but he went and stood next to it, hoping someone would come for him.

Lucy hovered around the slot machines until she worked up the courage to dive in. She knew real journalists just dove in. The first lady said she didn't give a damn about a mayor and threatened to burn Lucy with her cigarette if she didn't turn the camera off. She moved quick down the rows, and the patrons hissed at her. Some seemed kinda familiar like maybe people from high school but a little too old. She didn't talk to anyone from school anymore. She couldn't imagine there'd be a get-together next year for her class' twentieth, but she wouldn't go even if there was.

Curtis said he lost $40 in blackjack and was ready to try another place. "Blackjack has never been my game. With roulette, I know all the angles," he said. Lucy knew there were no angles.

She'd talked to twenty people total at Paradise and only two knew about Gottlieb. She set up her camera by the entrance and hit record. "This is Lucy, coming to you live from Paradise Casino. I spoke with patrons inside to get a feel for..." She could probably get a full five-minute segment out of it.

They started toward Horizon. Their pace was slow, and the casinos were further apart than they looked. They stopped at the same time.

"My knees are swelling up," Lucy said.

"Yeah, I probably shouldn't risk any more money."

"Maybe I already have enough people." She could just multiply it. Two out of twenty was the same as ten out of 100. Ten percent.

They turned around back toward Harrah's.

* * *

The next morning, Lucy had the idea that the survey should be in the *Gazette* too so more people would see it.

She was still building a viewer base for *Lucy on Laughlin*.

She found their copy of the cockfighting issue. The name of the guy who wrote the article was Ed Herman. There was a contact number for the paper at the bottom of the back page. She called, and it threw her off when Ed himself picked up after two rings.

"Ed, hey. Ed Herman?"

"This is Ed," he repeated.

"Hey, I'm a reporter too, from *Lucy on Laughlin*."

"What?"

"*Lucy on Laughlin*, it's my TV show. I'm Lucy."

"Hmm."

"I really liked your article about the cockfighting. I tried to interview Gottlieb about it, but he just walked away."

"Of course he did. He's a coward."

She told him about the survey story, and he laughed.

"I love it. It'll go on Thursday's front page."

"I thought the *Gazette* came out on Tuesdays."

"It used to. I just put it out whenever now." He said he'd mainly been producing the paper the past few years because people told him it couldn't last. "I can't compete with these tabloids. If there's another goddamn kidnapping, I swear to God..."

"It's crazy," Lucy said. "Our town is dying, but people care more about some rich little boy in Vegas."

"Yup. Oh well, fuck 'em. I'm going to keep making this paper until every casino is closed and I'm the only one left." It turned out that Ed was the *Gazette*. He'd had two employees at one point but had to let them go.

She thought he sounded lonely. She asked him about how blatant the cockfight had been, and he told her she should come see for herself.

"They're having another show on Saturday night," he said. "Twenty bucks at the door."

She told him she'd be there and said goodbye. Her stomach turned at the thought of watching roosters being forced to fight to the death, but it was happening whether she watched or not. Real journalists had to face ugly things head-on.

When Curtis got home from work, she told him about it.

"Another one? Oh my God," he said. "Cockfighting, wow. I can't imagine."

"Yeah, it's awful."

"You'd just never think you'd actually be able to see one live and in-person. I bet you can bet on them."

"It's like you're excited about it."

"No. I mean, it's messed up, but I dunno," he said and shrugged. "They're just mindless chickens. It's not like it's dogfighting or something."

* * *

Lucy put the tape in the VCR and connected the camcorder. She cut out the parts where the lady tried to burn her with her cigarette and the other lady threatened to throw her drink at her. The episode would be ready after she filmed the cockfights. Her show would be the only place you could see actual video.

She hadn't been inside GoldSky in over fifteen years, not since she turned 21 and could go to better casinos. They were really lax about carding people, so it was where underage kids went to party. As long as you were gambling, they'd keep bringing you whiskey and Cokes. Teenagers would sit at the cheap slot machines and make ten bucks last for hours.

She didn't know when it had closed down, hadn't noticed. It was a big brown office-looking building with mirrored windows. It didn't look like a casino aside from the flashing gold sign on the front. There were maybe eight cars in the parking lot when they pulled up. A cardboard sign was duct-taped to the entrance door: *Cockfights, $20 admission.* "Twenty bucks, shit," Curtis said.

"Ah, Ed didn't tell me about that," Lucy lied. Curtis put his hands on his hips and paced like he was really debating it, but she knew he was too excited to leave.

The doorman watched them closely and looked like he could just snap for no reason. He was short but built and had a pointed goatee. He wore black slacks and a tight black T-shirt like he was bouncing at a legit place.

Curtis circled back and handed him two twenties, and they went inside.

The lobby entrance was marble. "I can't believe they would just leave this marble here," Curtis said and crouched down and rubbed the ashy floor.

"Jesus, don't touch that."

"I mean, what's to stop someone from tearing it out and driving off with it. It just needs to be washed, and you could sell it for good money."

She kicked him soft. "Get up. Look, there's the ring." It was bigger and neater than she expected. It was a plywood octagon about fifteen feet wide and up to her chest. The ground inside was smooth patted-down dirt.

It was smoky from the ghouls staggered around the lobby. Curtis wandered past them and into the big game room, and Lucy stayed close by his side. It didn't seem like it had been abandoned all that long. The slot machines were gone, sold off probably, but the red felt tables were still there.

Curtis crouched down again and ran his fingers through the disgusting carpet. "The original green and yellow zigzag carpet," he said. "I don't think they ever changed it since I was a kid. You'd get that mildew smell even with all the smoke in the air." He was getting sentimental all of a sudden. Lucy knew the place meant a lot to him. He always went with his buddies in high school. She'd beg to tag along, but he always said they'd never let her in. She looked just like the little kid she was.

She looked up and saw that the men's eyes were on her. There was one standing by himself with a camera around his neck. The top of his head was bald, and the leftover hair on the sides was pulled back into a ponytail. She kicked Curtis a little harder this time. "C'mon."

She dove in like earlier at the slot machines. She went right up to Ed, and he started talking like they were already mid-conversation. "This town was originally supposed to be called Casino," he said.

"What?"

"Laughlin, they originally were gonna name it Casino, but Don Laughlin was too much of an egomaniac."

Lucy laughed.

"It's really not funny when you think about it," he said. "This town makes no sense in a depressed economy. What we should really do is just scrap the whole thing and go our separate ways."

You could tell he'd said this stuff a thousand times to anyone who'd listen. "It's not a bad idea," Lucy said. "I wanted to talk about the article a little bit."

"Oh, don't worry about it. It's already done. I'm putting it out tomorrow."

She was confused. He didn't have any details. He pulled a folded-up newspaper out of his back pocket and handed it to her. When she saw the headline, she laughed and didn't care about the details anymore.

BREAKING NEWS: LAUGHLIN HAS A MAYOR

"I can just picture his dumb face when he sees it," Ed said and smiled. Instead of Gottlieb's picture, there was a black silhouette. The article was very short and never actually said his name. It said out of hundreds surveyed, zero had heard of Gottlieb. Better this way, Lucy thought and folded it neatly and put it in her back pocket. Fuck him.

A bunch of guys around her age came all at once, and suddenly the lobby was packed, bodies pushing against bodies. They chain-smoked and passed around plastic handles of brown liquor. The room was impatient. They fought to get close to the ring.

Curtis was right in the middle of it, and a guy with sunglasses offered him his bottle. Lucy was jealous of how men seemed to become friendly without even talking. It was just being in the same place and nodding. Curtis took a pull off it, and she gagged for him. People started chanting, "Bring 'em out! Bring 'em out!" She felt dread like she was about to see something that would give her nightmares forever. She wanted to be next to her brother.

She pushed past people, saying, "Sorry, that's my brother right there," until she was behind him. She put her hand on his back, but he didn't notice. He was chanting along. The guys roared, and she stood on her tippy-toes. The first rooster had stepped through the fire exit door. He was black and orange, and a guy led him on a leash. Everyone yelled numbers and took out cash. They handed it to one guy who handed it to another guy. Nobody wrote anything down.

The black and orange cock stopped a few feet before the ring and wouldn't go any further. "See, he doesn't want to be here!" Lucy said. "They have to force him!" The guy with the leash picked him up and set him in the ring.

Everyone lost it when the next cock came out. He was pure white except for the long black feathers that sprouted out from his backside. He was bigger than the other one, and he strutted right up to the ring by himself, ready to go. A guy with bleach-blond hair and black stubble followed behind. He was young for the crowd, maybe thirty. He picked up the rooster and held him up to the crowd like a trophy. They went nuts and yelled out more bets.

"Jack," the guy with the liquor told them, shouting over the crowd. "Jack the Ripper. Undefeated." Lucy thought all roosters that were still alive were undefeated. She wanted to interview the guy before the match started. She fought to the front, this time more aggressive, putting her elbows into guys' ribs. They called her a bitch. She turned the camera on and pointed it at bleach-blond guy. He was kinda cute in a trashy way.

"Are you the owner of this rooster? What is your motivation to put him in harm's way?"

127

He gave her a confused look and pushed the camera away. "I'll smash that fucking camera," he said. The guys around Lucy turned against her and crowded her out. She retreated back to Curtis.

The blond guy was about to drop Jack in the ring when people turned around. There was some problem at the door. A man in a suit stepped past the angry bouncer, holding out the ID in his wallet. He had glasses and gray hair. It was Gottlieb. He put his hands on his hips like he expected something. Everyone looked back to Jack, impatient. Gottlieb stepped up closer to the ring and put his hands on his hips again, harder this time.

"He's the mayor," Lucy announced, but they just seemed confused. "Of Laughlin."

"That's right," Gottlieb said. "I'm the mayor of Laughlin, and trust me, you're gonna know my name!"

It wasn't until two cops burst in that everyone took off. They ran past the card tables towards the emergency exit. The blond guy was gone, and Jack the Ripper was loose. He arched his wings. He was beautiful and deserved so much more than to be a gladiator slave.

Lucy went after him. Her curly ponytail bounced, and dudes flew past her. She braced to get run over. Jack was freaking out, lashing out with his talons. She closed her eyes, bent over for him, and reached out. She got ahold of his feathers and one of his legs. He squawked and fought her, but she had him.

She made for the exit and felt the dry night air. "Put him down now, bitch!" someone yelled. She stopped and got a better hold of Jack, pinned down his wings and held him like a football. The blond owner was standing by the open door of an SUV. Lucy was out of breath. He ran towards her. She held tight to the rooster and took off again, not sure where she was going. She heard his footsteps closing on her fast. And then there were suddenly other footsteps.

The two people converged behind her at the same time. "Boom!" one of them yelled, and she heard a body thud on the ground. "Lucy! C'mon, keep running. Drop the chicken." It was Curtis. "I totally just lit that dude up. Did you see that shit?"

She felt her arthritis all at once. Her knees were on fire. Jack pecked on her hands hard, but she wasn't about to let go.

They got to the truck. "Did you see me light that dude up?" Curtis said again, huffing and puffing. "I saved you. What the hell are you doing with the rooster?" She was too out-of-breath to answer.

"Jesus Christ," he said. He was looking at the streams of blood running down her arms. "There's goddamn razor blades attached to his legs!" he said and pointed. Just above Jack's feet were shiny sickle-looking blades, held on with electric tape.

"Those sick bastards," Lucy wheezed out.

"Just leave him on the ground and let's go."

"No way," she said and tossed Jack into the back of the cab.

"If he tears up my seats, I swear to God."

She tried to calm Jack down while Curtis drove, but he kept flapping his huge wings, and her blood got everywhere, and he did tear up the seats a little.

* * *

"Ah man, I feel woken up," Curtis said, pacing the living room. "Like really awake, ya know? For the first time in forever. I just saw that dude going after you, and I reacted. It was just instinct like they talk about."

"I saw the chance to rescue him, so I took it," Lucy kept saying, her bloody arms wrapped in paper towels.

She had Curtis hold Jack down while she unwrapped the electric tape and took off the razor blades. "Hurry up. He's fucking strong," he said. "How's he so strong?" When he let go, Jack charged at him and chased him out the back door and into the yard.

Lucy walked up to Jack slowly, and he let her pick him up. He knew she'd saved him. She took him back inside, and Curtis cautiously followed.

"It's so cruel what they make him do," she said and set him down.

"We gotta get rid of him," he said.

"I won't abandon him." She'd risked her life for him. She was bleeding for him.

Curtis sighed and flopped onto the couch. "He *is* beautiful. Jack the Ripper," he said and smiled. "The way he struts cracks me up. The undisputed champion. You saw how he came up to the ring. He knew what was going on, and he loved it. You took that away from him."

"Don't say that. It's just because he knows no other life."

"Can you imagine living like him?" he said. "Wild. Any day could be his last. I bet he appreciates every meal more than we ever could. A real soldier."

It was quiet. She thought about it. "We're not guaranteed another day either," she said. "I'm serious.

Think about JonBenét. A beauty queen. Thought she had her whole life ahead of her and then—" She snapped her fingers. She picked up the *Enquirer* from the coffee table and pointed at little Henry on the cover. "Four years old. Had everything going for him, then—" She snapped her fingers again.

"Yeah."

"Who knows how much longer we have? We gotta get out of Laughlin while we still can."

"I dunno," he said and leaned back. "It's not so bad. What do you wanna leave for?"

"To be a cameraman for *Cops*."

He laughed.

"I'm serious. My reel is getting really solid."

"But what about your arthritis?"

"They have medicines. I'll be on partial disability, and I'll have Medicare, and I'll lose weight. For training, I'm gonna run up hills with my camera on my shoulder."

He ran his hand over his face. "Fuck it, sure. You could be a *Cops* cameraman."

"Yeah. In Vegas. They film in Vegas."

* * *

Curtis had already left for work the next morning when Jack started crowing. He'd be quiet just long enough for Lucy to start to drift off, then he'd startle her all over again. She got up, squinting, and stepped in something wet on the kitchen tile. She didn't see him until he crowed right by her ear and made her jump. He was perched on top of the fridge.

She took him outside and wondered if there was a way

131

you could sever a rooster's vocal cords without hurting him too bad. Her eyes were all the way open when they went back inside. There was piss on the kitchen tile with little brown swirls of shit. There was a note on the counter— *Clean up this shit*.

Jack followed her around everywhere she went in the house, and she had to close the bathroom door behind her fast to keep him from coming in. She was still sore, and he was restless. She figured he was used to training every day. He had to be hungry. Roosters ate seeds or corn feed or something. She gave him Wonder Bread, and he picked the slices apart.

She needed to train, even if she was sore. She remembered in *Rocky* when he chases the chicken and finally catches it. She took Jack to the backyard and ran at him, but he wouldn't run from her.

* * *

When Curtis got home that afternoon, he threw the new *Gazette* in her lap. "Read that!" he said.

LAUGHLIN MAYOR ABDUCTED BY COCKFIGHTING RING, PROBABLY DEAD

There was a big picture of Gottlieb.

"Oh my God!" she said. "Wow, oh my God!"

"Man, we gotta just drop Jack off in front of GoldSky. We never should've fucked with these people."

"This is huge." The biggest story in the history of Laughlin. She went to the kitchen phone. She had to talk to

132

Ed. He didn't pick up the first time or the second time. She left a voicemail the third time, telling him to get back to her as soon as possible.

"I'm taking him back," Curtis said and went for Jack.

"Jack! Don't let him!" she yelled, and Jack squawked and his feathers stood up. "Just calm down for two seconds," she told Curtis.

He sat on the couch and pouted. She read the article. There weren't many details. It said when the mayor's wife got home from visiting her parents in Arizona, Gottlieb was gone, and there was a ransom note on the counter. He'd been kidnapped by "a local mafia that specializes in cockfighting." They wanted $10,000.

"Those were some real gangsters we were with," Curtis said. "Real mafia guys."

Lucy had rubbed elbows with thugs and come out on top. She looked at Jack. That's what it took to be a crime journalist. She could probably infiltrate groups and get inside access. The cockfighting guys just didn't seem all that dangerous or organized. The article didn't totally make sense. "Did they sign the letter, *Sincerely, the cockfighting guys?*"

"God, what do you think they'd do to us if they found us with Jack?" he said.

She tried Ed again. He picked up this time and acted like he didn't remember who she was.

"He was kidnapped for real?" Lucy asked.

"Looks that way."

"Have you seen the letter? We should work together on this. It's too big of a story for just one person."

"I dunno. We'll see."

"Why didn't you mention me in the article? I did the survey."

"What?"

She said it again.

"It wasn't in there?"

She hung up so she wouldn't cuss him out. "Fuck Ed," she said.

"What happened?"

"We gotta go talk to the mayor's wife."

"What? No. We gotta give Jack back then lay low. Can you grab him? He won't let me near him."

"I'm not gonna lay low."

"What?"

"I'm not gonna lay low. I need to talk to the mayor's wife." She got out the yellow pages and found Gottlieb. A woman picked up and said hello in a quivering voice. Lucy introduced herself and heard the woman whispering to men in the background.

"Hey Lucy, this is Terry with the Police Department." She remembered Terry from school. He was in Curtis' grade. "We gotta keep this line open. We're gonna have a press conference tomorrow at 5 p.m. and we'll answer any questions we can then." He hung up without letting her talk.

They were startled by someone banging on the door. Curtis looked terrified. The person could see Lucy in the kitchen through the window. It was the bleach-blond guy. She went to answer.

"Don't!" Curtis said.

"He already saw me." She went and opened the door. There were two other guys standing by Curtis' F-250. One

134

was the angry bouncer. Their SUV was parked on the street.

"Hey there," Lucy said, trying to sound calm.

"Where's my rooster?" he said.

"Rooster like a male chicken?"

"Shut the fuck up. Go get Jack now or we'll set this truck on fire."

"Okay. Lemme just go get him right now." He was asleep on the kitchen floor when she picked him up. "I'm so sorry, buddy. I have no choice. Your dad is a lunatic. I hope you never lose."

When Jack saw his owner, he got excited like he'd missed him. The guy snatched Jack from her arms and baby-talked him. He went and put him in the SUV then opened the driver's side door and looked for something. Lucy's pulse quickened. He walked back to her with something in his hand. She was frozen and couldn't close the door.

The guy threw it on the front porch. It was a newspaper, the new *Laughlin Gazette*.

"That shit right there. That shit has nothing to do with us. You're a reporter. Tell your friend Fred or Ed or whatever the fuck his name is, we'll kill him if ever says shit about cockfighting again."

"Okay. I don't care what you do to him though," she said. "He's not my friend."

The guy went and got in the SUV, but the stout bouncer still stood in the driveway. He turned to the truck and took out a knife.

"Please no," Lucy said. "It's our only car."

He stopped and looked up at her and smiled. He bent down and stabbed a tire. It hissed, and he took his time slashing the other three too. He got in the SUV, and they

135

took off and held their middle fingers out the windows.

* * *

Lying in bed, Lucy was surprised to hear the toilet flush at nine the next morning. It was Monday, and she'd assumed Curtis got a ride to work. She got up and stood outside his bedroom door for a minute and listened, but he didn't make any noise. "Going to the press conference now," she said. "Just gonna walk." There was some rustling but nothing else.

She couldn't let Ed have exclusive coverage. She took two ibuprofens and stretched, trying to touch her toes but not getting close. The press conference wasn't for another three hours, but she didn't know how long it was gonna take to get there. The address was on Oasis Way. That was in Oasis Plains, the neighborhood where everyone with money lived.

It was hotter that day than it had been. She moved slow and alternated hands for pulling the cart. She was pale and should've put on sunscreen. She didn't go outside enough. She was gonna make it. She'd tell this story in her interview with Fox.

She saw Longview Ave. way ahead. It would eventually get her to the strip. She heard something behind her but kept her gaze down. It got closer, and she turned her head and saw the big body of Curtis moving down the street. His eyes were at his feet too.

He gradually caught up until he was leading the way.

"How much further to the strip, you think?" Lucy said. It still wasn't in sight.

"Another few miles," he mumbled back.

She wanted to apologize about the tires again but thought that would annoy him. "Did you call in to work?"

"Yeah. Told them I pulled my back."

Her body felt wrecked by the time they got to the strip and passed Paradise. She started crying from the pain. Curtis took the cart and put his arm around her. She cried and he held her up while they walked. She knew it was like that time an Olympic runner hurt his leg during a race and his father came out of the stands to help him finish, pushing past security personnel. He cried on his dad's shoulder. Lucy was crying about all types of stuff.

They both were broken and wobbly when they got to the house, but Lucy tried to not let it show. There was a podium in the front yard, the same one the mayor used in the park. A state trooper was talking to Terry. Mrs. Gottlieb must've lent it to them.

Ed was the only other person there. Lucy set up her camera, and Ed pretended not to notice her. She pointed her camera at him and wondered if he could've done it. The trooper looked at his watch and said he'd give it another minute. Some neighbors worked their way out of their houses and into their patio furniture to watch. They were old.

The trooper shrugged his shoulders and stepped to the podium. "Guess no one else is coming." Lucy turned the camera to him. She could tell he couldn't wait to leave Laughlin. "Two days ago, the wife of Evelyn Gottlieb...Gottleeb?" he said and looked to the mayor's wife, but she was bawling. "Two days ago, the mayor's wife came home to find a troubling letter. Based on this letter we believe that the

137

mayor has been abducted by a local mafia-like organization."
He paused and let it sink in. He's terrible at this, Lucy
thought.

Ed took pictures of the newly widowed woman, and
Lucy wondered again, *Why not Ed?* He hated the mayor
and would do anything for a story.

"Mayor Gottlieb has been fearlessly spearheading
a campaign against a criminal organization involved in
cockfighting and...drugs too?" Terry shrugged. The state
trooper continued, "The letter leads us to believe that these
are the same individuals responsible for..."

"Can you read the letter out loud?" Lucy asked.

The trooper held his finger out. "I will open up the
floor to questions at the end. Right now, I want to give the
mayor's wife the opportunity to speak to the kidnappers."

She was a frail woman with lots of pearls and diamonds
on her. Her hair was dyed jet black. She made her way to the
podium, her hands clasped together. She grabbed the sides
of the podium and tried to get it together. Lucy couldn't
imagine. As she took a deep breath, the front door of the
house stirred. Everyone turned. The doorknob rattled, and
Terry crouched down and got his gun out.

Mayor Gottlieb stepped out of the house. There he
was, alive. He waved his arms. "Forget it." He was scruffy
and wearing sweats. "This whole goddamn town!"

"Tom?" His wife said and fell to his feet. "You escaped!"
She wrapped her arms around his legs.

"I've been in the attic the whole time," he said. "I wrote
the goddamn letter." His wife let go and looked up at him
wild. Lucy kept the camera steady on them.

"I'm sorry, honey. I just...what's wrong with this

138

town?" he cried. "I mean, why does nobody care about anything or anybody?" Mrs. Gottlieb punched him from the ground, hitting his legs.

"You scoundrel!" She got up and swung for his head, but Terry held her back. Ed was rolling in the grass, laughing and slapping the lawn. He kept taking pictures.

The state trooper told Gottlieb to put his hands behind his back. "You're under arrest for..." He didn't know the name of the crime.

"Being a dickhead," Ed said, and the trooper told everyone to shut up. Lucy had the only video footage of this. She thought it could be expanded into an hour-long special.

"I think it's time to leave here," Curtis said.

"What do you mean?" she said. "This is incredible stuff."

"No. I mean, like, move away." He looked sad.

Gottlieb muttered to himself as they put him in the back of the cruiser. Lucy felt bad for him. Before the trooper shut the door, she bent down, and pain shot up from her lower back. She met his gaze. "I'm sorry, Mayor. Don't take it personal," she said. "It's not your fault. It's Laughlin. I mean, they were gonna call it Casino."

Ride With Me

I'm tracking my pizza on the Papa John's website. When it says "On the Way," I watch out the window until an old beater pulls up. A tall guy steps out with shaggy hair spilling out of his ball cap. He's wearing slacks and a red polo. He comes up the walkway, and I see that he's young, younger than me, maybe 23, 24. He knocks on the door, and I wait a second to answer, make it seem like I was doing something else. Then I open up and let him smell the weed. He looks exhausted, but a smirk comes to his lips. I ask him if this is his last delivery even though I already know it is. I wait until places are almost closed then order something. He didn't expect the question. He's shy and cute, looks like a snack. "Yeah, last one," he says and looks down.

I ask if he wants to smoke a bowl. He laughs and looks back at his car then at the ground again. He wants to, I can tell, but he's not sure it's worth hanging out with me. I'm not a pretty girl, but a lot of guys don't care about that. "C'mon," I say and wave him in. I go to the couch and leave the door open behind me. It takes a second, but he eventually comes in, and I tell him to set the pizza on the coffee table. He sits on the opposite end of the couch. I can smell his sweat. It's summer on the Texas coast, and it's hot no matter what time it is.

I let him have the first hit since I'm already stoned, and he lets out a sigh as he exhales. He says thanks, he needed that. I ask him if he's heard the podcast, *Serial*, the one about Hae Min Lee's murder. He says he remembers when it was big a few years ago but never listened. It's crazy how many people have never heard it, big as it was. The people who did hear it don't want to talk about it anymore, don't remember the details. It's 2019 and I just heard it for the first time, and I wanna talk about it now. "I'm so jealous of you," I tell him. "I wish I could hear it for the first time again. Wanna listen to the first episode? I'm gonna put it on." When you smoke someone out, they kinda have to sit there and listen to you. They have to watch and listen to what you want. Sometimes they get up and leave, but most feel like they have to hang out awhile.

The host, Sarah Koenig, introduces Adnan Syed, Hae's ex, who's in prison for her murder. "Did he do it?" the delivery guy asks, and I shush him.

"Just listen." Koenig talks about how Adnan may have had an alibi that wasn't brought up in trial. A girl named Asia says she saw him at the school library at the time the murder allegedly took place.

"So he's innocent?" he says. I see his nametag for the first time—*Sean*. I explain that when I first heard this

142

episode I swore he was innocent, but then I watched this analysis on YouTube by this attorney. He said surely dozens of people would've seen him that day after school if he was really there. Why would only one remember? Isn't it more likely Asia is mistaken about what day it was? Researching the case is all I do now since I got my settlement.

"Huh?" Sean says. He spaced out. It's frustrating. The munchies come on, and I remember the pizza. It's still in the thermal pouch thing that keeps it warm. I ask him if he's sure he doesn't want a slice, and he says he's sure—he's so sick of the stuff. I eat two or three slices then scoot closer to him. I lean in for a kiss, but he moves his head back. I expect him to get up and leave, but he doesn't, and that's a sign. I see that little cup of garlic sauce that comes with Papa John's, and I ask him if he'd like to eat it out of my pussy. I regret this right away, but I get lucky and he laughs. I go along with it and laugh too even though I was serious. I struggle with different urges and say things as soon as they pop into my head. My appetites are mixed up, the wires crossed.

I ask Sean if his girlfriend is gonna wonder where he is, and he tells me he doesn't have one. If he didn't like me at least a little bit, he would've lied. I load another bowl and ask him what he thinks so far.

"I dunno. He sounds innocent." He really does. He says all the right things. I decide I like Sean enough to go to my bedroom and get the coke out of my underwear drawer. I don't ask him if he's down. I just start cutting up small lines on the coffee table. More people like coke than you'd think. Most people won't seek it out, but they won't turn it down either.

I put on the second episode, and it talks about how

all of Adnan's friends say he was a great guy and that he actually took the breakup with Hae well. He just wanted her to be happy. That said, there's also an entry in Hae's journal where she says he won't accept that she dumped him.

After a couple bumps, Sean starts talking, and I'm glad he's feeling more open and comfortable. He says he can't wait to quit this job. "My boss is a prick," he says, and I tell him I know what he means. I've had so many shitty bosses. Just three months ago at Whataburger, before my grease accident, I had to deal with my manager talking to me like I was a baby or something. Now I don't have to worry about work for at least another year.

"That must be nice," Sean says. "I mean, not having to worry about money for a while." I can tell the weight of the world is on his shoulders. He keeps talking, and I feel bad for him, but it starts to annoy me because he's talking over the podcast, whining about people who don't tip.

"Hold on," I say, cutting him off. "Listen to this part."

It says several people overheard Adnan ask Hae for a ride that day. According to Jay, the accomplice and the state's star witness, Adnan strangled Hae in her car and put her body in the trunk. Adnan denies ever asking for a ride or being in Hae's car that day.

"He's lying," Sean says. "He's guilty."

"It definitely doesn't help his case," I say. I can tell he's into it now. He's slouched on the couch, staring at the ceiling, listening intently. We take a few more bumps and crush the episodes. There was a tight window between when school let out and when Adnan supposedly called Jay from Best Buy to tell him he'd killed Hae and needed to be picked up. Adnan said it wasn't possible, but Koenig tested it out and was just able to make it to Best Buy in time. She also compared Adnan's call record to Jay's story and said the phone was most likely in the park later that night based on which cell towers were pinged. The park is where Jay said they buried Hae.

"He did it," Sean says. "That piece of shit." He punches the couch cushion. It's kinda hot how worked up he's getting about it.

"But Jay could've done it alone and pinned it on Adnan," I say and put my hand on his knee. "They both agree that Jay borrowed Adnan's car and cell phone that day." This seems to throw Sean off.

"Jay's story is so inconsistent," he says. My hand moves to his thigh. "I mean, if I was telling the truth, my story would never change." He looks down at my hand. "I need to shower."

"You can just shower here," I say. "There's clean towels in there." I keep the bathroom ready for guests. I take him by the hand to the bathroom. He thanks me and closes the door, and I know he wants to stay the night.

Once I hear the water running, I go outside and look at his car. The windows have that cheap tint on them that peels easy. I cup my hands around my face and peek inside. There's a sleeping bag in the backseat and clothes piled on the floorboard, more Papa John's polos. I imagine him trying to sleep in the backseat, his long legs scrunched up, sweating in the humid night.

I go back inside and wait for him, and he comes out of the bathroom with no shirt and his hair still dripping like he's in a hurry. His torso is lean, and he has a bad farmer's tan, and I could just eat him up. "I was thinking while I was

145

in there," he says, pulling on his shirt. "I really think Jay did it alone."

"Maybe," I say. "But what about the Nisha call?" I couldn't get around it. During a time that Adnan claims he was at school and Jay had his phone, there was an outgoing call to a girl named Nisha. Adnan was sort of dating her, and she was someone Jay didn't know, so it couldn't have been Jay who called her. It puts Adnan with Jay around when the murder took place.

Sean puts his hands on his hips, squints his eyes. He sits down on the couch and looks me dead in the eye. "I don't care," he says and points at my laptop. "That man is not a murderer."

"You've heard him talk on a few podcasts and you think you know him?"

He gets up and steps away then turns back to me. "Don't tell me what I know and don't know." This is our first fight. I tell him his emotions are clouding his judgment.

"It was a butt dial," he says. That was Adnan's excuse. He said Nisha's number was programmed into the phone, and it could've accidentally dialed while it was in Jay's pocket.

"How convenient," I say. He doesn't say anything for a minute, just looks pissed.

"So you think he's guilty."

"I just don't know," I say. "And honestly I don't feel like I can go on until I do. It's killing me."

"Same." He sounds sad now.

We're quiet. I do another bump. "It's tough when we can only hear their voices, you know?" I say.

"Yeah."

146

I can usually tell when people are full of shit. I just have to look them in the eye. "If I could just talk to Jay face-to-face," I say.

"Yeah, I'm really good at reading people," Sean says.

I give him a look, and I know he knows what I mean. I smile. "So we're going to Baltimore?"

"I don't see any other way," he says. "Fuck but I've got work tomorrow."

"Fuck that job. Fuck your manager. I've got money."

"For real? Yeah!" he says and gets hyped up. He takes off his Papa John's polo and tries to tear it and throws it on the ground. We're going to Baltimore, and we're not coming back until we know the truth. "We're leaving in twenty minutes," I announce. I grab random clothes and stuff them in a backpack. I grab the weed and the coke and the pizza.

We get in my Corolla and get on the interstate. I have Sean cut up lines on the center console.

"How far is Baltimore from Corpus?" he asks.

"Google says 24 hours, but we can do it in a lot less." We're restless, just want to be there. I want to walk through the halls of Woodlawn High School to get a feel for it. I need to time how long it takes to get to Best Buy.

"He just sounds so innocent," Sean says.

"Yeah. It's almost too perfect though," I say. "Like it's an act. Like, you couldn't design a better innocent-sounding guy."

We agree that if Adnan did it, he's a true sociopath. If he did it, he planned it out. It wasn't a crime of passion where he snapped. And then the lying about it for years.

"What if Jay is the sociopath though?" Sean says. The lawyer lady on *Serial* said that she's never met the

147

stereotypical charismatic sociopath in all her years and that the odds are insane that Koenig would meet one on her first try. I googled sociopathy though, and the Wikipedia article says 2% of the general population are sociopaths. That's a lot of people.

Driving up the coast, we go over the same questions over and over. If Jay did it alone, what was his motive? What about the lack of physical evidence? Sean keeps talking. That's the problem sometimes with coke—you talk too much and don't pick up on other people's body language. I give him short answers and don't feed into it. "I mean, if I killed my girlfriend, I wouldn't say I don't remember that afternoon," he says. "I'd have a specific story."

He stops there. He's run out of things to say, and it's finally quiet. I suddenly feel exhausted. I take a big bump, but it doesn't do much. My brain is out of dopamine. I fight to keep my eyes open. I haven't slept in like 24 hours.

We're out of coke by the time we get to the Houston suburbs where we stop to get gas. I ask Sean if he can take over driving. "I'm crashing hard," I say.

"Me too." He looks like shit.

"I wish we could just like teleport there," I say.

"Yeah."

We sit there at the gas pump and don't say anything. I think about my bed, and I wonder how much taking care of a boy like this costs. We go into the 7-Eleven and buy Monster energy drinks. He takes the keys from me and starts the car.

"If we head back now, I can still make my shift tonight."

"Are you serious?" I say, but I'm glad he said it. We're linked up. He stares out the window.

"Listen, the more I think about it, I'm not sure it was a butt dial."

"So you think he did it," I say.

"I wouldn't say that. I dunno. I mean, it's always the boyfriend or husband."

"Yeah, usually." I scratch his back. "Let's get you home."

"It's just messed up, ya know? I know I don't really know you, but I would never strangle you and bury you in a park like that, no matter what."

Our eyes meet, and I go in for a kiss, and he doesn't pull away, but he doesn't move his lips. He cracks his Monster open, and we pull out of the gas station. I try to keep him company, but I'm fading. The silence feels easy with him, and I want to tell him how, sometimes when I'm alone in the house, I shit my pants on purpose and just sit in it for a while. I think better of it though and drift off as we ride with the bay on our shoulder.

Acknowledgments

These stories first appeared
in the following publications:

Joyland "Lexapro"
Reprinted in *2022 Short Story Advent Calendar*
The Opiate "Tilikum Gets Loose"
Mystery Tribune "Monticello"
Maudlin House "Inside Recess"
Faded Out "You're Gonna Know My Name"

Thank you for everything: Dad, Collin, Claire Christoff, Chris Vanjonack, Jon Nix, Shelley Imholte, Huff Stuff, Alex Shakar, David Wright, Amy Hassinger, Ted Sanders, S. Kirk Walsh, Jen Sy, Mary Miller, Ashleigh Bryant Phillips, Oliver Zarandi, John Dermot Woods, Elle Nash, Michael Hingston, Mallory Smart, Roman Reigns, and Nick Garza.

About the Author

Drew Buxton is a writer and social worker from San Antonio, Texas. His writing has appeared in, among others, *Joyland*, *The Drift*, *Electric Literature*, *Vice*, *Ninth Letter*, and *Vol. 1 Brooklyn*.

You can find him online at drewbuxton.com and on Instagram @drew.buxton.